FRANK AMONG THE RANCHEROS

HARRY CASTLEMON

1st WORLD
LIBRARY
Literary Society

Frank Among The Rancheros

Harry Castlemon

© 1st World Library – Literary Society, 2006
PO Box 2211
Fairfield, IA 52556
www.1stworldlibrary.org
First Edition

LCCN: 2006905706

Softcover ISBN: 1-4218-2135-4
Hardcover ISBN: 1-4218-2035-8
eBook ISBN: 1-4218-2235-0

Purchase *"Frank Among The Rancheros"*
as a traditional bound book at:
www.1stWorldLibrary.org/purchase.asp?ISBN=1-4218-2135-4

1st World Library Literary Society is a nonprofit organization dedicated to promoting literacy by:

- Creating a free internet library accessible from any computer worldwide.
- Hosting writing competitions and offering book publishing scholarships.

Readers interested in supporting literacy through sponsorship, donations or membership please contact:
literacy@1stworldlibrary.org
Check us out at: www.1stworldlibrary.ORG
and start downloading free ebooks today.

Frank Among The Rancheros
contributed by Tim, Ed & Rodney
in support of
1st World Library Literary Society

CONTENTS

CHAPTER I

A NOVEL BATTLE

"Pull him along, Carlos! Pull him along!" shouted a young gentleman about sixteen years of age, as he danced about on the back porch of his uncle's house, in a state of great excitement; "why don't you pull him along?"

"He'll come, after awhile," replied the person addressed; "but he is very wild and obstinate."

The boy on the porch was almost beside himself - so much so, in fact, that he found it utterly impossible to stand still. He was jumping wildly about, swinging his arms around his head, and laughing and shouting at the top of his lungs.

We have met this young gentleman before. We have been with him through the woods, accompanied him across the prairie, and seen him in some exciting situations; but, for all that, it is by no means certain that his most intimate friend, could he have beheld him while he was dancing about on the porch, would have recognized him. The last time we saw him he was dressed in a suit of blue jeans, rather the worse for wear, a slouch hat, and a pair of heavy horseman's boots. Now, he sports a suit of clothes cut in the height of fashion - that is, Mexican fashion. They are not exactly of the description that we see on the streets every day, but they are common among the farmers of Southern California, for that is where this young gentleman lives. He is dressed in a short jacket of dark blue cloth, trimmed around the edges, and on the sleeves, with gold lace, and wide trousers of the same material, also gaudily ornamented. The hat, with which he fans his flushed face, is a sombrero, bound with gold cord, the ends of which are adorned with tassels, that fall jauntily over the edge of the brim. An embroidered shirt of gray cloth, and shoes and stockings, complete his attire; or, we may add, a long crimson sash, which is wound several times around his waist, and tied at the side, and a pair of small Mexican spurs, whose rowels are ornamented with little silver bells, which tinkle musically as he moves his feet about. If you fail to recognize an old acquaintance in this excited, sunburnt boy, you surely can call the name of the tall, broad-shouldered, sober-looking youth, who stands at his side. Three months in the saddle have not changed Frank Nelson a great deal, only he is a little more robust, and, perhaps, more sedate. He has lost none of his love of excitement, and he is quite as interested in what is going on before him as Archie; but he stands with his hands in his pockets, looking as dignified as a judge. It would be a wonder if they were not somewhat excited, as they are witnessing a desperate battle that is going on between two of their uncle's Rancheros and a wild steer, which one of them has lassoed, and is trying to pull through the gate into the cow-pen. The animal is struggling furiously for his freedom, and the issue of the contest is doubtful.

At the time our story begins, Frank and his cousin had lived two months in Southern California, where Mr. Winters owned a farm - or, in the language of that country, a *rancho* - of sixteen thousand acres. Besides attending to his business in the mines, and superintending his affairs in Sacramento, Uncle James had devoted a portion of his time to stock-raising; and, when Frank and Archie first saw his immense droves of horses and cattle, they thought them sufficient in numbers to supply all the markets in America.

Mr. Winters's rancho was not managed like the farms in our part of the country. To begin with, there were but three fences on it - one inclosed two small barns and corn-cribs; another, a pasture of two or three acres, and the third formed the cow-pen. In the barns, Uncle James kept his riding and farm horses; the pasture was for the use of the half dozen cows which supplied the rancho with butter and milk; and the cow-pen was nothing more nor less than a prison, into which, in the spring of the year, all the young cattle and horses were driven and branded with the initials of the owner's name. This was done so that Mr. Winters and his hired men might be able to recognize the stock anywhere. The cattle sometimes strayed, and became mixed up with those of the neighbors, and the marks on their flanks showed to whom they belonged.

A fence around that farm would have been useless. None of the cattle and horses had ever been handled, except when they were branded, and, consequently, they were very wild. Sometimes they became frightened and stampeded; and then they behaved like a herd of buffaloes, which turn aside for nothing, and stop only when they are completely tired out. On these occasions, the strongest fences that could have been made would have been trampled down like the grass beneath their feet.

Of course, these cattle and horses had never seen the inside of a stable. Indeed, a barn large enough to accommodate them would have been an immense building, and would have cost more money than all the stock-raisers in the country were worth. However, there was no need of shelter for them. The grass on the prairie was abundant at all seasons of the year, the winters were very mild, and the cattle were always fat and in condition to be driven to market.

All this stock was managed by half a dozen men, called Rancheros. Four of them were Mexicans; the others were our old friends, Dick Lewis and Bob Kelly. So skillful were these men in their business, that a herd of cattle, which, in the hands of any one else, would have proved utterly unmanageable, was driven about by them with perfect ease. Sometimes it became necessary to secure a single member of these droves. Perhaps the housekeeper wanted some fresh meat for dinner, or Uncle

James desired a new riding horse; in either case, the services of these men were invaluable. Mr. Winters would issue the necessary orders to Carlos - who was the chief of the Rancheros, and the man who managed the farm during the absence of his employer - and an hour or two afterward four quarters of fine beef would be carried into the cellar, or Mr. Winters would be requested to step to the door and see if they had captured the horse he wanted. The Rancheros accomplished this with their lassos, which they carried suspended from the horns of their saddles wherever they went. A lasso is a long rope, about as large as a clothes-line, and is generally made of rawhide. One end of it is fastened to the saddle, and the other, by the aid of a strong iron ring, formed into a running noose. This contrivance these herdsmen could use with a skill that was astonishing. Mounted on their fleet horses, they would ride up behind a wild steer, and catch him by the horns, around his neck, or by one of his feet, as suited their fancy.

On the morning we find Frank and Archie on the porch, their nearest neighbor, also a stock-raiser, had ridden over to inform them that one of his fine steers, which he had intended to drive to market, had escaped from his Rancheros, and joined one of Mr. Winters's droves; whereupon Frank, who, in the absence of his uncle, acted as the head man of the ranch, sent for Carlos, and commanded him to capture the runaway, and confine him in the cow-pen until his owner should send for him. Carlos had obeyed the first part of the order, but just then it seemed that that was all he could do. The steer had suddenly taken it into his head that he had been driven far enough, and that he would not go through the gate that led into the cow-pen; and, although Carlos pulled him by his lasso, which he had thrown over his horns, and another Ranchero, named Felix, vigorously applied a whip from behind, the obstinate animal refused to budge an inch. Sometimes he would kick, and plunge, and try to run off; and then the horse on which Carlos was mounted, which seemed to understand the business quite as well as his master, would plant his fore-feet firmly on the ground to stop him. Finding that he could not effect his escape in that way, the steer would run around in a circle; and the horse would turn around also, keeping his face toward the animal all the while, and thus avoid being wrapped up in the lasso. This novel battle had been going on for nearly ten minutes, and even Frank had become highly excited over it.

"Pull him along, Carlos!" shouted Archie, jumping about on the porch as if he had lost all control over his legs, and they would dance in spite of every thing he could do to prevent it. "Pull him along! Whip up behind, Felix; hit him hard!"

Archie continued to shout his orders at the top of his voice; but they did not seem to help the matter any, for the steer still refused to move. He had fallen to his knees, and laid his head close to the ground, as if he had deliberately resolved that he would remain there; and for a long time, all the pulling and whipping the two Rancheros could do, brought nothing from him but angry snorts and shakes of the head.

"Now, Archie," said Carlos, as he stopped to wipe the big drops of perspiration from his face, "what would you do with this fellow?"

The boys, who never neglected an opportunity to pick up items of information concerning every thing that came in their way, had been taking lessons of the Rancheros in horseman-ship, throwing the lasso, and managing wild cattle; and Carlos thought this a proper occasion to ascertain how much they remembered of what they had learned.

"Well," replied Archie, pulling off his sombrero, and digging his fingers into his head, to stir up his ideas, "I'd keep pulling and hauling at him until I got him tired out, and then I think I could manage him."

"That would take up too much time," said Carlos; "I've got other work to do, and I am in a hurry."

"Make your lasso fast to the horn of your saddle, and start up your horse, and drag him in," suggested Frank.

"That's the idea, and that's just what I'm going to do," said Carlos.

But that was just what the Ranchero did *not* do. While he was preparing to put this plan into operation, the steer suddenly jumped to his feet, and made another desperate attempt to effect his escape, and this time he was successful. There was a loud snap, Carlos's heels made a flourish in the air like the shafts of a windmill, and, in an instant, he was stretched at full length on the ground. His saddle-girth had parted, and the steer was at liberty to take himself off, which he did in short order.

The boys gazed in astonishment at the fallen horseman, who righted himself with alacrity, stretched his arms and legs to satisfy himself that there were no bones broken, and then commenced shouting some orders to his companion, who put spurs to his horse and started in pursuit of the steer, which was galloping over the prairie, dragging Carlos's saddle after him. He was very soon overtaken, and Felix, raising himself in his stirrups, swung his lasso around his head once or twice, to make sure of an accurate aim, and launched it at the steer. The lariat whistled through the air, as true to its course as a ball from a rifle, the noose settled down over his horns, the horse stopped suddenly, and the runaway lay struggling on the ground.

His last attempt at escape seemed to have exhausted his energies, for when he had regained his feet, he allowed Felix to lead him back to the gate and into the cow-pen, where he was turned loose, to remain until his owner should send for him.

Harry Castlemon

CHAPTER II

FRANK'S NEW HOME

Frank and Archie, as we have before remarked, had been in California about two months; and, between riding, hunting, visiting, and assisting Uncle James, who was engaged in selling off his stock and closing up his business, preparatory to his return to Lawrence, they had passed the time most agreeably. They were as fond as ever of excitement, were almost constantly in the saddle, and Mr. Winters often said that if they and their horses and dog did not travel a thousand miles every day, it was not because they did not try.

When the boys first arrived in California, they thought themselves expert in all manner of frontier accomplishments. But one morning, they rode over to visit Johnny Harris and Dick Thomas - two boys, about their own age, with whom they had become acquainted - and, during the day, they witnessed some feats of skill that made them wonder. Johnny and Dick, to show what they could do, captured and rode a couple of wild horses, that had never been handled before; and Frank and Archie were compelled to admit that they had some things yet to learn. Every boy in that country could throw the lasso, and the cousins found that, if they desired to keep up their reputation, they must put themselves under instructions. Dick and Bob readily took them in hand, and, although the boys were awkward at first, they improved rapidly. They soon learned to throw the lasso with considerable skill, and Frank speedily took the lead in rifle-shooting, while Archie began to brag of his horsemanship. The former could bring a squirrel out of the top of the highest oak on the farm, at every shot; and his cousin could bend down from his saddle and pick up his sombrero from the ground, while his horse was going at the top of his speed.

The horses the boys rode were the same that had carried them across the prairie, and they were now hitched at the end of the porch, saddled and bridled, and awaiting the pleasure of their masters. One of them, Sleepy Sam, looked as sleepy as ever. He stood with his head down, and his eyes half closed, as if it made no difference to him whether Archie took his morning ride or not. The other, a magnificent iron-gray, pulled impatiently at his halter, and pranced about, apparently as much excited as Archie had been a few moments before. This was the "king of the drove" - the one the trappers had captured during their sojourn at the Old Bear's Hole. He answered to the name of Roderick; for Frank had read Sir Walter Scott's "Lady of the Lake," and, admiring the character of the rebel chieftain, had named his favorite after him. Perhaps the name was appropriate, for the animal sometimes showed a disposition to rebel against lawful authority, especially when any one besides Frank attempted to put a saddle or bridle on him. He was a wild-looking fellow, and he had a way of laying back his ears, and opening his mouth, when any one came near him, that would have made a stranger think twice before trying to mount him. With Frank, however, he was as gentle as a dog. He would come at his call, stand on his hind legs, and carry his master's whip or sombrero. He would kick and bite at Frank when the latter tickled him in the ribs, all in sport, of course; but if Mr. Winters, or one of the herdsmen, came about him, he would use his teeth and heels in good earnest. He was as swift as ever, and Frank had yet to see the horse that could beat him.

The saddles these horses wore were like every thing else about themselves and masters, of the Mexican pattern. They were made of beautifully-stamped leather, with high pommels in front, the tops of which were flat, and as large around as the crown of Frank's sombrero. A pair of saddle-bags was fastened across the seat of each, in which the boys carried several handy articles, such as flint, steel, and tinder for lighting a fire; ammunition for their revolvers, which were safely stowed away in bearskin holsters strapped in front of the saddles, and large clasp-knives, that were useful in skinning squirrels when the boys went hunting. Behind the saddles, neatly rolled up, and held in their places by straps, were a couple of pouches, which they used in rainy weather. They were pieces of India-rubber cloth, with holes in the center for the wearers' heads. They were large enough to afford complete protection from the rain, and could also be used as tents in case the boys found it necessary to camp all night on the prairie.

We have spoken of Frank's dog; but were we to let the matter drop here, it would be slighting an animal which had played a somewhat important part in the history of Frank's life in California. His name was Marmion, and he had been presented to Frank by Captain Porter - an old fur-trader, who lived a few miles distant from the rancho, and with whom the cousins were great favorites. Archie did not like the dog, and, if the truth must be told, the dog had not the smallest particle of affection for Archie. In fact, he cared for no one except his master, and that was the reason the fur-trader had given him to Frank. He was as large as two ordinary dogs - very courageous, and so savage that no one cared to trouble him. He had seen some stirring times during his life, and his body was covered with wounds, some of which were not entirely healed. Frank was quite as fond of him as he was of Brave, and with good reason, too. Marmion had received those wounds while fighting for his master, and it was through his interference that Frank had been saved from a long captivity. It happened before the commencement of our story, and how it came to pass shall be told in the following chapters.

The house in which Frank and Archie lived stood in a grove of stately oak-trees, and, externally, was in perfect keeping with its surroundings. It was built of massive logs, in the form of a hollow square, with an open court in the center, which was paved with stone. The windows, which extended down to the floor, and which were used for ingress and egress quite as often as the doors, were protected by shutters made of heavy planks, and there were four loop-holes on each side of the house, showing that it had been intended to serve as a defense as well as a shelter. Indeed, it looked more like a fortification than a dwelling.

The house was old, and had a history - an exciting one, too, as any one could have told after examining it closely. The walls bore numerous scars, which had been made by bullets, and the trees surrounding the dwelling were marked in the same manner. The grove had not always been as peaceful and quiet as we found it. Its echoes had been awakened by the yells of infuriated men and the reports of hostile rifles, and the very sod upon which Frank sometimes stretched himself after dinner, to while away an hour with some favorite author, had been wet with blood.

When the house was built, there was not another human habitation within a circle of twenty miles. The country was an unbroken wilderness. Mr. Winters's nearest neighbors were bands of roving freebooters, who robbed all who came in their way. They did not, however, content themselves with waylaying solitary travelers. They frequently made organized attacks upon remote farm-houses, and one night they made a sudden descent upon Mr. Winters's rancho. But the old frontiersman had lived too long in that country, and was too well acquainted with the character of his neighbors, to be caught napping. He and his Rancheros were armed to the teeth, and prepared for a fight; and, after a siege of two days, during which time the robbers poured an almost constant shower of bullets against the walls of the house, they withdrew, after shooting and dispersing the cattle, and destroying the crops. Not one of Mr. Winters's party was injured; but the outlaws suffered so severely, that they never repeated the attempt to rob that rancho.

Frank and Archie never grew tired of hearing Uncle James tell the story of that fight, and nearly every day they examined the marks of the bullets on the logs, sometimes being foolish enough to wish that they had been there to take part in those exciting scenes, or that the robbers would return and make another attack on the house, so that they might be able to say that they had been in a real battle. Then they should have a story to tell that would be worth listening to. They never imagined that, before they were many years older, they could recount adventures quite as exciting as their uncle's.

The interior of the house presented a strange contrast to the outside. When one crossed the threshold, he found himself surrounded with all the comforts of civilization. There were fine carpets on the floors, oil paintings on the walls, and easy chairs, sofas, and musical instruments in abundance. The room the boys occupied was the only one in which could be found any traces of the backwoods. It was a pleasant, cheerful apartment, quite as nicely furnished as the other rooms in the house, and every thing about it bespoke the taste and character of its young masters. A stranger, having taken a single glance at the numerous articles hung upon the walls, and scattered about over the floor - some of them useful and ornamental, others apparently of no value or service to any one - could have told that its presiding geniuses were live, wide-awake, restless boys.

The room contained a fine library, an extensive collection of relics of all descriptions, and its walls were adorned with pictures, only they were of a different character from those in the other parts of the house. Frank and Archie cared nothing for such scenes as the "Soldier's Dream" and "Sunrise in the Mountains;" their tastes ran in another channel. Their favorite picture hung over their writing desk, and was entitled, "One Rubbed Out." In the foreground was a man mounted on a mustang that was going at full speed. The man was dressed in the garb of a hunter, with leggins, moccasins, and coonskin cap, and in one hand he carried a rifle, while the other held the reins which guided his horse. The hunter was turned half around in the saddle, looking back toward half a dozen Indians, who had been pursuing him, but were now gathered about their chief, who had been struck from his horse by a ball from the hunter's rifle. The latter's face wore a broad grin, which testified to the satisfaction he felt at the result of this shot. This picture had been shown to old Bob Kelly, who, after regarding it attentively for a few moments, declared that it must have been painted by some one who was acquainted with the story of his last trip to the Saskatchewan, the particulars of which he had related to Dick on the night he made his first appearance in their camp.

"I don't know how the chap that made that ar' pictur' could have found it out," said old Bob, who, simple-hearted fellow that he was, really believed that the hunter in the painting was intended to represent him, "'cause I never told the story to nobody 'cept you an' my chum Dick. But thar's one thing wrong about it, youngsters. When I shot a Injun, I didn't hold my rifle on the horn of my saddle, an' waste time laughin' over it. I loaded up again to onct, an' got ready for another shot."

At the opposite end of the room hung a picture of a hunters' camp. Two or three men were stretched out on the ground before a cheerful fire, resting after the labors of the day, while others were coming in from the woods - some loaded with water-fowl, some with fish, and the two who brought up the rear were staggering under the weight of a fine deer they had shot. Archie often wondered where that camp could have been located. He did not believe there was a place in the United States where game of all kinds was as abundant as the hunters in the picture found it.

Paintings of this character occupied prominent places on the walls of the room, and between them hung numerous relics the boys had collected during their journey across the prairie, and a few trophies of their skill as hunters. Over the door were the antlers of the first and only elk they had killed, and upon them hung a string of grizzly bear's claws, which had once been worn as a necklace by an Indian chief, and also a bow, a quiver full of arrows, a stone tomahawk, and a scalping-knife - all of which had been presented to them by Captain Porter. At the head of the bed were two pairs of deer's horns fastened to the wall, and supporting their rifles, bullet-pouches, powder-horns, and hunting-knives.

These articles were all highly prized by the boys; but, upon a nail driven into the wall beside the book-case, hung something that, next to his horse and dog, held the most exalted place in Frank's estimation. It was the remnant of the first lasso he had ever owned. He thought more of it than of any other article he possessed, and he would have surrendered every thing, except Roderick and Marmion, before he would have parted with that piece of a rawhide rope. It had once saved his uncle's life; and, more than that, Frank himself had been hanged with it. Yes, as improbable as it may seem, one end of that lasso had been placed around his neck, the other thrown over the hook which supported one of his large pictures, and Frank had been drawn up until his toes only rested on the floor; and all because he refused to tell where he had hidden a key. Where the rest of the lasso was he did not know. The last time he saw it, it was around the neck of a man who was running through the grove at the top of his speed, with Marmion close at his heels. The dog came back, but the man and the piece of lasso did not; and this brings us to our story.

CHAPTER III

TWELVE THOUSAND DOLLARS

One day, about six weeks before the commencement of our story, Frank and Archie were sent to San Diego on business for Uncle James. When they returned, they found a new face among the Rancheros - that of Pierre Costello, a man for whom Frank at once conceived a violent dislike. Pierre was a full-blooded Mexican, dark-browed, morose, and sinister-looking, and he had a pair of small, black eyes that were never still, but constantly roving about, as if on the lookout for something. His appearance was certainly forbidding; but that was not the reason why Frank disliked him. It was because Marmion regarded him with suspicion, and seemed to think he had no business on the rancho. When the Ranchero came about the house, Marmion would follow him wherever he went, as if he feared that the man was about to attempt some mischief; and, when Pierre returned to his quarters, the dog always seemed to be immensely relieved. Frank invariably made common cause with his favorites, whether they belonged to the human or brute creation, and without taking the trouble to inquire into the merits of the case; and, when he found how matters stood between Pierre and Marmion, he at once espoused the cause of his dog, and hated the Ranchero as cordially as though the latter had done him some terrible injury, although the man had never spoken to him, except to salute him very respectfully every time they met.

That Pierre hated and feared the dog, quite as much as the

animal disliked him, was evident. He would scowl, and say "*Carrajo*," every time Marmion came near him, and lay his hand on his knife, as if it would have afforded him infinite pleasure could he have found an opportunity, to draw it across the dog's throat. Frank had often noticed this, and consequently, when he one day came suddenly upon the dog, which was looking wistfully at a piece of meat Pierre was holding out to him, he was astonished, and not a little alarmed. The Mexican scowled, as he always did when Frank came near him, and walked away, hiding the meat under his coat.

"Give it to me, Pierre," said Frank; "Marmion don't like to be fed by strangers."

The Ranchero kept on as if he were not aware that he had been spoken to; and his conduct went a long way in confirming the new suspicions that had suddenly sprung up in Frank's mind.

"Uncle," said he, that evening, after supper, as he joined Mr. Winters and Archie, who had seated themselves on the porch to enjoy the cool breeze of evening, "how long do you intend to keep that new Ranchero?"

"As long as he will stay," replied Mr. Winters. "He is one of the most faithful men I ever had, and he is quite as skillful in his business as either Carlos or Dick."

"He is a mean man for all that," said Frank; "he tried to poison Marmion, to-day."

"I don't blame him," said Archie; "a meaner, uglier dog I never saw" -

"Now, Archie," interrupted Frank, "I like the dog; and even if I didn't, I would keep him because he is a present."

"How do you know that Pierre tried to poison him?" asked Mr. Winters.

"Why, he was holding a piece of meat out to the dog, and when I came up he walked off in a great hurry," replied Frank, who, when he came to state the case, found that it was not quite so strong against the Ranchero as he had at first supposed.

"He may have done all that, and still be innocent of any desire to injure your favorite. Marmion doesn't like him, and, no doubt, Pierre is trying his best to make friends with him. I'll insure your dog's life for a quarter."

Frank was far from being satisfied. Somehow, he did not like the scowl he had often seen on Pierre's face. He was certain that the Ranchero had intended to harm Marmion; but why? Not simply because he hated the dog, but for the reason that the animal was in his way. This was the view Frank took of the case; and, believing that Pierre was there for no good, he resolved to keep a close watch on all his movements.

A day or two after that, Mr. Winters and Archie set out on horseback for San Diego, the former to collect the money for a drove of horses he had sold there, before his departure for the East, and Archie to explore the city. Frank, hourly expecting his two friends, Johnny Harris and Dick Thomas, who had promised to spend a week with him, remained at home, with the housekeeper and two of the Rancheros, one of whom was Pierre, for company. Dick and Bob, and the rest of the herdsmen, were off somewhere, attending to the stock.

Frank, being left to himself, tried various plans for his amusement. He read a few pages in half a dozen different books, took a short gallop over the prairie, shot a brace of quails for his dinner; all the while keeping a bright lookout for his expected visitors, who, however, did not make their appearance. About noon, he was gratified by hearing the sound of a horse's hoofs in the court. He ran out, expecting to welcome Johnny and Dick, but, to his disappointment, encountered a stranger, who reined up his horse at the door, and inquired:

"Is this Mr. Winters's rancho, young man?"

Frank replied that it was.

"He is at home, I suppose?" continued the visitor.

"No, sir; he started for the city early this morning."

The gentleman said that was very unfortunate, and began to make inquiries concerning the road Mr. Winters generally traveled when he went to San Diego - whether he took the upper or lower trail - and then he wondered what he should do.

"My name is Brown," said he; and Frank knew he was the very man his uncle expected to meet in San Diego. "I owe Mr. Winters some money for a drove of horses I bought of him before he went to the States, and I have come up to pay it. I have here twelve thousand dollars in gold," he added, laying his hand on his saddle-bags, which seemed to be heavy and well filled.

"Couldn't you remain until day after to-morrow?" asked Frank. "Uncle James will be at home then."

"I can't spare the time. I am on my way to Fort Yuma, where I have some business to transact that may detain me three or four days. I don't like to carry this money there and back, for it is heavy, and there is no knowing what sort of travelers one may meet on the road. Wouldn't it be all right if I should leave it here with you?"

"Yes, sir," replied Frank, eager to accept the responsibility; "I can take care of it. But I thought you might want a receipt."

"I am not particular about that. Mr. Winters has trusted me for about six months, and I think I can afford to trust him for as many days. I'll call and get the receipt when I come back."

As Mr. Brown said this, he dismounted, and Pierre, who, ever since his employer's departure, had seemed to have nothing to do but to loiter about the house, and who had stood at the opposite side of the court, listening to every word of the conversation, came up to hold his horse. The visitor shouldered his saddle-bags, and followed Frank into a room which went by the name of "the office," where Mr. Winters transacted all his business. The room was furnished with a high desk, a three-legged stool, and a small safe, which, like those in banks, was set into the wall, so that nothing but the door could be seen.

"That is just the place for it," said Mr. Brown; "it will be secure there."

"But I haven't got the key," replied Frank; "uncle always carries it in his pocket."

"Well, I don't suppose there would be any danger if you were to leave the money on the porch. Of course, your hired people can be depended on, or your uncle wouldn't keep them."

Frank thought there was at least one person on the rancho who could not be trusted to any great extent; but, of course, he said nothing about it. He glanced around the room, wondering what he should do with the money, when he discovered that his uncle had left the key of the desk in the lock. For want of a better place, Frank decided to put the gold in there. Mr. Brown took it out of his saddle-bags, and packed it away in the drawer - six bags in all, each containing two thousand dollars, in bright, new "yellow-boys." Then, declining Frank's invitation to stay to dinner, the gentleman bade him good-by, mounted his horse, and resumed his journey.

"Twelve thousand dollars!" said Frank, to himself, as he locked the desk and put the key into his pocket. "Why, that's a fortune! Now that I think of it, I almost wish Mr. Brown hadn't left it here. What would Uncle James say if somebody should break into the house and steal it?"

As Frank asked himself this question, he turned suddenly, and saw Pierre standing on the porch, in front of one of the windows, watching him with eager eyes. He must have moved very quietly to have approached so near without attracting the boy's attention, and that, to Frank, whose suspicions had already been thoroughly aroused, was good evidence that the Ranchero was not just what he ought to be. If he was an honest man, he would not try to slip around without making any noise.

Finding that he was discovered, Pierre removed his sombrero and said, without the least embarrassment:

"Is it your pleasure to ride? If so, I will saddle your horse."

"You need not trouble yourself," replied Frank, rather gruffly. "I shall remain at home."

Pierre bowed and walked away.

"Now, that rascal thinks he is sharp," said Frank, gazing after the Ranchero. "He never offered to saddle my horse before, and he wouldn't have done it then if I hadn't caught him looking in at the window. I wonder if he thinks I am foolish enough to ride for pleasure at this time of day, with the thermometer standing a hundred degrees in the shade? That fellow is a scoundrel, and he is up to something. Perhaps he is after this gold. If he is, he may have the satisfaction of knowing that he won't get it."

So saying, Frank began to close and fasten the shutters which protected the windows, and while thus engaged, he caught a glimpse of the Ranchero's dark face peering at him around the corner of the house.

"If I owned this ranch," said Frank, to himself, "that fellow shouldn't stay here five minutes longer. I'd pay him off, and tell him to leave as fast as his horse could carry him."

Having satisfied himself that the windows were so well secured that no one could effect an entrance through them, Frank opened the drawer and took another good look at the money, as if he were afraid that it might have been spirited away even while he was in the room; after which he locked the desk, and hid the key under the edge of the carpet. Then glancing about the office, to make sure that every thing was safe, he closed the door, and hurrying into his own room, he threw the key under his writing-desk, next to the wall. Then he breathed easier. The money was as safe as it would have been in the bank at San Diego.

CHAPTER IV

FRANK PROVES HIMSELF A HERO

"There!" said Frank, with something like a sigh of relief. "If Pierre gets into that office to-night, he'll have to use an ax; and if he tries that" -

Frank finished the sentence by shaking his head in a threatening manner, and taking down his rifle, which he proceeded to load very carefully. He had made up his mind to fight, if it should become necessary.

He was now more anxious than ever for the arrival of his two friends, for he did not like the idea of remaining alone in the house all night, with so much money under his charge, and a villainous-looking Mexican hovering about. Frank, as we know, was very far from being a coward; but having by some means got it into his head that Pierre was a rascal, and that something unpleasant would happen before morning, he could not help feeling rather anxious.

The afternoon wore slowly away, but Johnny and Dick did not make their appearance. Darkness came on apace, and Frank, being at last satisfied that he was to be left alone in his glory for that night at least, ate his supper, and visited Roderick in his stable to see that he was well provided for, and then whistled for his dog, which he had not seen since the departure of Mr. Brown. Marmion, however, did not respond to the call. Frank whistled and shouted several times in vain, and then set out to hunt up his favorite. He visited the Rancheros' quarters, and found Felix and Pierre sitting in the door of one of the cabins, smoking their cigarettes. The former had not seen the dog; but, willing to serve Frank to any extent in his power, offered to go in search of the animal. Pierre, however, said that would be useless, for he had seen Marmion in hot pursuit of a rabbit. No doubt he had driven the game into its burrow, and was engaged in digging it out. When he caught the rabbit, he would come home of his own free will.

Although Frank was suspicious of every thing Pierre said or did, he could see no reason for disbelieving this story. Marmion was quite as fond of the chase as his young master, and frequently indulged in hunting expeditions on his own responsibility; sometimes being absent all day and nearly all night. But he was not off hunting then, and Pierre had told a deliberate falsehood, when he said that he had seen him in pursuit of a rabbit. The Ranchero had determined upon a course of action which he knew he could not follow out so long as the dog was at liberty, and Marmion was, at that very moment, lying bound and muzzled under one of the corn-cribs, almost within hearing of his master's voice.

Frank slowly retraced his steps toward the house, feeling more nervous and uneasy than ever. In Marmion he had an ally that could be depended on in any emergency; and, if the dog had been at his side, he would have felt perfectly safe. But he was not the one to indulge long in gloomy thoughts without a cause, and in order to drive them away, he lighted his lamp, and, drawing his easy-chair upon the porch, amused himself until nine o'clock with his guitar. The music not only served to soothe his troubled feelings, but also had the effect of banishing his suspicions to a great extent, and left him in a much more cheerful frame of mind.

"How foolish I have been," said he, to himself. "Because Pierre is ugly, like all the rest of his race, and because he always carries a knife in his belt, and hates Marmion, I have been willing to believe him capable of any villainy. I don't suppose

Harry Castlemon

he has thought of that gold since he saw me lock it up."

As Frank said this, he pulled his chair into the room, and selecting Cooper's "Last of the Mohicans" from the numerous volumes in the library, he dismissed all thoughts of the Ranchero, and sat down to read until he should become sleepy. He soon grew so deeply interested in his book, that he did not hear the light step that sounded on the porch, nor did he see the dark, glittering eyes which looked steadily at him through the open window. He saw them a moment afterward, however, for, while he was absorbed in that particular part of the fight at Glen's Falls, where Hawk-Eye snapped his unloaded rifle at the Indian who was making off with the canoe in which the scout had left his ammunition, a figure glided quickly but noiselessly into the room, and stopped behind the boy's chair.

"Now, my opinion is that Hawk-Eye was not much of a backwoodsman, after all," said Frank, who was in the habit of commenting upon and criticising every thing he read. "Why did he leave his extra powder-horn in his canoe, when he knew that the Hurons were all around him? You wouldn't catch Dick or old Bob Kelly in any such scrape, nor me either, for that matter, for I would" -

Frank's soliloquy was brought to a close very suddenly, and what he was about to say must forever remain a secret. His throat was seized with an iron grasp, and he was lifted bodily out of his chair, and thrown upon the floor. So quickly was it done that he had no time to resist or to cry out. Before he could realize what had happened, he found himself lying flat on his back, and felt a heavy weight upon his breast holding him down.

Filled with surprise and indignation, he looked up into the face that was bending over him, and recognized Pierre Costello, whose features wore a fiendish expression, the effect of which was heightened by a murderous-looking knife which he carried between his teeth. Scowling fiercely, as if he were trying to strike terror to the boy's heart by his very appearance, he loosened his grasp on Frank's throat, and the latter, after coughing and swallowing to overcome the effects of the choking he had received, demanded:

"What do you mean, you villain?"

Pierre, without making any reply, coolly proceeded to overhaul the contents of Frank's pockets. Like all boys of his age, our hero was supplied with a variety of articles, which, however serviceable they may be to a youngster of sixteen, no one else could possibly find use for, and the Ranchero's investigations brought to light a fish-line, bait-box, a rooster's spur, of which Frank intended to make a charger for his rifle, a piece of buckskin, half a dozen bullets, a brass cannon, a pocket comb, a quill pop-gun, a small compass, a silver ring, a match-box, a jack-knife, and a piece of lead. These articles he tossed upon the floor, rather contemptuously, and then turned all Frank's pockets inside out, but failed to discover any thing more.

"Where are they?" demanded Pierre, removing the knife from his mouth, and looking savagely at his prisoner, who all this time had lain perfectly still upon the floor, apparently not the least alarmed.

"Where are what?" inquired Frank.

"The keys, you young vagabond!" returned the Ranchero, astonished at the result of his search, and in a great hurry to get through with his business. "The keys that open the office and the safe. Speak quick!"

"The safe key is where you'll never get your hands upon it," replied Frank. "If you want it, you'll have to go to San Diego, catch Uncle James, and throw him down, as you did me, and search his pockets for it. But that is something a dozen such fellows as you couldn't do."

"But the office key! Where's that?"

"It's in a safe place, also," said Frank, who had already resolved that the would-be robber should never learn from him where he had hidden the key. "If I were a man, I should like to see you hold me down so easily. Let me up, or I'll call for help!"

"If you speak above your breath, I'll choke you!" said Pierre, with savage emphasis. "I am not done with you yet! Is the money in the safe?"

"That's none of your business! Let me up, I say! Here, Marmion! Marmion!"

"*Carrajo!*" muttered the Ranchero, again seizing his prisoner's throat in his powerful fingers. "Do you want me to kill you?"

Frank, nothing daunted by this rough treatment, struggled manfully, and tried hard to make a defiant reply, but could not utter a sound. Pierre tightened his grasp, until it seemed as if he had deliberately resolved to send him out of the world altogether, and then released his hold, and waited until Frank was able to speak before he said:

"You see that I am in earnest! Now, answer me! Is the gold in the safe?"

"I am in earnest, too!" replied Frank, as bravely as ever. "I shall not tell you where it is. Are you going to let me up?"

"I am going to make you tell where you have put that key!" said Pierre, as he removed the sash his prisoner wore around his waist, and began to confine his arms behind his back. "If I once get inside the office, I'll soon find out where you have put that gold."

"But you are not inside the office yet, and I don't think you will get there very soon. If you were well acquainted with me, you would know that you can not drive me one inch. You're a coward, Pierre," he added, as he released one of his hands by a sudden jerk, and made a desperate but unsuccessful attempt to seize the ruffian by the hair. "You don't give a fellow a fair chance. I wish my dog was here."

"You need not look for him," said the Ranchero; "he'll never come."

Frank made no reply. He was wondering what his captor intended to do with him, and turning over in his mind numerous wild plans for escape. Pierre, in his haste, was tying the sash in a very clumsy manner, and Frank was certain that, with one vigorous twist, he could set himself at liberty. In spite of his unpleasant and even painful situation - for, after his attempt to catch the Ranchero by the hair, the latter had turned him upon his face, and was kneeling upon him to hold him down - he could not help chuckling to himself when he thought how he would astonish Pierre if he did not mind what he was about.

"Perhaps he will leave me, and try to force an entrance into the office," soliloquized Frank. "If he does, I am all right! I'll jerk my arms out of this sash, pick up that rifle, and the first thing Mr. Pierre Costello knows, he'll be the prisoner. I'll march him to the quarters, and tell Felix to tie him, hand and foot."

Unfortunately for the success of these plans, the Ranchero did not leave the room after he had tied Frank's arms. He was too well acquainted with the old house to think of trying to force an entrance into the office. He knew that the doors and window-shutters were as strong as wood and iron could make them, and that it would be a dangerous piece of business to attempt to break them open. Felix, all unconscious of what was going on in the house, snored lustily in his quarters, and the housekeeper slept in a room adjoining the kitchen; and if Pierre awakened either of them, he might bid good-by to all hopes of ever securing possession of the gold. His only hope was in compelling Frank to tell where he had put the office key.

"Now, then," said he, "I will give you one more chance. Where is it?"

"Where's what?" asked Frank.

"The office key!" exclaimed the Ranchero, enraged at the coolness of his prisoner. "Tell me where it is, or I'll drive you through the floor!"

As he said this, he raised his fist over Frank's head, as if he were on the point of putting his threat into execution.

"Drive away!" replied Frank.

"Then you won't tell me where it is?" yelled the Ranchero.

"No, I won't! And when I say no, I mean it; and all the threats you can make won't scare me into saying any thing else!"

Pierre hesitated a moment, and then jumped to his feet, his actions indicating that he was determined to waste no more words. He placed his knife upon the table, closed the windows, and dropped the curtains, so that any one who might happen to pass by could not see what was going on in the room. His next action was to seize Frank by the collar of his jacket, and pull him roughly to his feet, preparatory to putting into operation his new plan for compelling him to tell where he had hidden the office key.

"If you conclude to answer my question, let me know it," said the Ranchero.

"I will," was Frank's reply.

Pierre stepped upon a chair, and removing one of the pictures from its hook, tossed it upon the bed. After that, he took Frank's lasso down from the nail, beside the book-case, and holding the noose in his hand, threw the other end over the hook.

Frank had thus far shown himself to be possessed of a good share of courage. He had bravely endured the choking, and had made defiant replies to all Pierre's threats; but when he saw this movement, he became thoroughly alarmed. He knew what was coming.

"Aha!" exclaimed the Ranchero, who had not failed to notice the sudden pallor that overspread the boy's countenance; "Aha!"

"What are you going to do?" asked Frank, in a trembling voice.

"Can't you see?" returned the Ranchero, with a savage smile. "I told you that I was going to make you tell me where you had put that office key, didn't I? Well, I intend to do it. I have tamed many a wild colt, and I know how to tame you!"

As he spoke, he adroitly threw the noose over Frank's head, and drew it tight around his neck. Then, seizing him by the shoulders, he pushed him against the wall, under the hook, and pulled down on the lasso, until Frank began to rise on his toes. This was intended merely to give him a foretaste of what was in store for him.

"Now you know how it feels," said Pierre, slackening up on the rope, "and you ought to know, by this time, that I am not playing with you. I am in sober earnest, and if you don't answer my question, I'll hang you, right here in your own room, and with your own lasso. This is your last chance! Where's that key?"

Frank hesitated.

CHAPTER V

THE FIGHT IN THE COURT

Frank was certainly in a predicament. He had his choice between revealing the hiding-place of the office key, and being hanged with his own lasso - a most disagreeable alternative. On one side was a lingering death, and on the other, something of which Frank stood almost as much in awe - disgrace. Never before had so heavy a responsibility rested upon him; and if he lost that money, what other evidence would be needed to prove that he was not worthy of being trusted?

"Come, come!" exclaimed the Ranchero, impatiently. "Are you going to answer my question?"

"I don't know whether I am or not," replied Frank. "Don't be in such a hurry. Can't you give me time to think about it?"

"You have had time enough already," growled Pierre. "But I'll give you two minutes more, and while you are thinking the matter over, you can bear one thing in mind: and that is, if you don't tell me where that office key is, you'll never see daylight again."

The expression on Pierre's countenance told Frank that the villain meant all he said.

Frank leaned his head against the wall, closed his eyes, and made use of those two minutes in trying to conjure up some plan to defeat the robber. He had not the slightest intention of allowing him to put his hands on that money if it were possible for him to prevent it, and he was wondering if he could not make use of a little strategy. If he could invent some excuse to get Pierre out of the room for a few moments, he was sure that he could release his hands. Would it not be a good plan to tell him where he had hidden the key, and while Pierre was in the office searching for the gold, free himself from his bonds, and seize his rifle, and make the villain a prisoner? Wouldn't it be a glorious exploit, one of which he could be justly proud, if he could save the twelve thousand dollars, and capture the Ranchero besides? Frank thought it would, and determined to try it.

"Pierre," said he, "if I tell you where that key is, what will you do?"

"*If!*" exclaimed the Ranchero; "there are no ifs or ands about it. You must tell me where it is."

"But what I want to know is, what will you do with me?"

"I promise you, upon the honor of a gentleman, that no harm shall be done you."

"Gentleman!" sneered Frank. "The State's prison is full of such gentlemen as you are. If I were trying to rob a man of a few cents, I'd never think of calling myself a gentleman."

"Now, just look here," said Pierre, "if you think you can fool me, you were never more mistaken in your life. A few cents, indeed! I heard all that passed between you and Mr. Brown, and I know that there are twelve thousand dollars somewhere in that office. I call it a fortune. It is much more than I could ever earn herding cattle, and I am bound to have it. Where's that key?"

"You must answer my question first," said Frank. "If you had the key in your hand now, what would you do with me?"

"Well, as I am not fool enough to give you the least chance for escape, the first thing I should do would be to tie you hard and fast to that bed-post. Then I'd take the gold, mount my horse, and be off to the mountains."

"And leave me tied up here?" exclaimed the prisoner.

"Exactly. Felix, or the housekeeper, would release you in the morning."

This answer came upon Frank like a bucket of cold water. His fine plan for releasing himself and capturing the robber would not work. The latter saw his look of disappointment, and laughed derisively.

"I am too old," said he, "to allow a boy like you to play any tricks upon me. You won't tell me where the key is, then?"

"No, I won't. If that money was mine, you might take it, and I would run the risk of catching you before you could get very far away with it. But it belongs to my uncle; you have no claim upon it, and, what's more, you sha'n't touch it."

"Is that your final answer?" asked the Ranchero, bracing himself for a strong pull. "You had better ponder the matter well before you decide. What do you suppose your uncle will think, when he comes home and finds you hanging to this hook? He had rather lose the money a thousand times over than to part with you."

Frank shuddered as the Ranchero said this, and, for the first time, he felt his firmness giving away. But he was possessed of no ordinary degree of fortitude, and, after a momentary thrill of terror, his courage returned, and he looked at Pierre as bravely as ever.

The Ranchero paused for a moment or two, to give his last words time to have their full effect, and then said: "Once more - yes or no."

"No, I tell you," was the firm reply. Scarcely were the words out of his mouth, when the Ranchero began to pull down upon the lasso, and Frank, in spite of his desperate struggles, was drawn up until he almost swung clear of the floor. Pierre held him in this position for a few seconds - it seemed an age to Frank, who retained his consciousness all the while - and then gradually slackened up on the lasso, until his prisoner's feet once more rested firmly on the floor. Frank reeled a moment like a drunken man, gazed about him with a bewildered air, and attempted to raise his hands to his throat, while the Ranchero stood watching him with a smile of triumph.

"I have given you one more chance," said he. "Have you come to your senses yet."

Frank tried in vain to reply. The choking he had endured had deprived him of his power of utterance, but it had not affected his courage or his determination. There was not the least sign of yielding about him.

Pierre had thus far conducted his operations with the most business-like coolness, and in much the same spirit that he would have exhibited had he been breaking one of Mr. Winters's wild horses to the saddle. He had smiled at times, as he would have smiled at the efforts of the horse to escape, and the thought that he should fail in his object had never entered his head. He had been certain that he could frighten or torture Frank into revealing the hiding-place of the office key; but now he began to believe that he had reckoned without his host. He was astonished and enraged at the wonderful firmness displayed by his prisoner. He had never imagined that this sixteen-year-old boy would prove an obstacle too great to be overcome.

"You are the most obstinate colt I ever tried to manage," said Pierre, in a voice choked with passion; "but I'll break one of two things - your spirit or your neck; it makes no difference to me which."

Without waiting to give his prisoner time to recover his power of speech, the Ranchero wound the lariat around his hands, and was about to pull him up again, when he was startled by the clatter of a horse's hoofs in the court.

The sound worked a great change in Pierre. As if by magic, the savage scowl faded from his face, and he stood for an instant the very picture of terror. All thoughts of the twelve thousand dollars, and the vengeance he had determined to wreak upon his prisoner, were banished from his mind, and gave place to the desire to escape from the house as secretly and speedily as possible.

"Who can that be?" he muttered, dropping the lasso, and throwing a frightened glance ever his shoulder toward the door.

"I'm sure I don't know," said Frank, speaking with the greatest difficulty; "and I don't care who it is, if he will only make a prisoner of you."

The Ranchero scowled fiercely upon his plucky captive, hesitated a moment, as if he had half a mind to be revenged upon him before he left the house, and then, catching up his knife, and extinguishing the lamp, he jerked open one of the windows, and disappeared in the darkness.

Frank was no less astonished than delighted at his unexpected deliverance. He tried to shout, to attract the attention of the unknown horseman, but all his efforts were unavailing. His attempts to release his hands, however, which he commenced the instant the Ranchero left the room, were more successful. Pierre's carelessness in tying the knots was a point in his favor then; for, in less time than it takes to record the fact, Frank was free. He threw the noose off his neck, pulled the lasso down from the hook, and hastily coiling it up in one hand, he ran to the place where he had left his rifle, fully determined that the robber should not escape from the ranch without an attempt on his part to capture him. His rifle was gone. The

Ranchero had caught it up as he bounded through the window, thinking he might find use for it, in case he should happen to run against the visitor in the dark.

Frank looked upon the loss of his rifle as a great misfortune; for, not only did he believe the weapon lost to him forever, but he was powerless to effect the capture of the Ranchero, even if he succeeded in finding him. However, he did not waste time in vain regrets. He sprang through the window, and, running around the house, entered the court, to look for the horseman whose timely arrival had saved his life. He went as far as the archway that led into the court, and there he suddenly paused, and the blood rushed back upon his heart, leaving his face as pale as death itself. He had told the Ranchero that a dozen such men as he could not overcome his uncle; but the scene before him belied his words. Flat upon his back, in the middle of the court, lay Mr. Winters, with Pierre Costello kneeling on his breast, one hand grasping his victim's throat, and the other holding aloft his murderous-looking bowie, whose bright blade glistened in the moonlight like burnished silver.

Frank started back, rubbed his eyes, and looked again. There could be no mistake about it, for the moon shone brightly, rendering all the objects in the court as plainly visible as if it had been broad daylight. He was not only terribly frightened, but he was utterly confounded. He had believed Mr. Winters to be fast asleep in his bed at the hotel in San Diego; but there he was, when Frank least expected him, and, more than that, he was being worsted in his struggle with Pierre. The boy could not understand it.

"Unhand me, you scoundrel!" he heard Uncle James say, in a feeble voice.

"Not until you have given me the key of the safe," was the robber's answer. "I have worked hard for that gold to-night, and I am not going to leave the ranch without it."

Then commenced a furious struggle, and Frank turned away

his head, lest he should see that gleaming knife buried in his uncle's body.

Never before had Frank been so thoroughly overcome with fear. He had just passed through in ordeal that would have tried the nerves of the bravest man, and he had scarcely flinched; but to stand there a witness of his uncle's deadly peril, believing himself powerless to aid him, was indeed enough to strike terror to his heart.

"O, if I only had my rifle, or one of my pistols!" cried Frank, "wouldn't I tumble that villain in a hurry? Or if I could find a club, or could loosen one of these stones" -

Frank suddenly remembered that he held in his hand a weapon quite as effective at short range, when skilfully used, as either a rifle or pistol. It was his lasso; and, until that instant, he had forgotten all about it. Then the blood flew to his cheeks; his power of action returned, and his arms seemed nerved with the strength of giants. How thankful was he, then, that his desire to become as expert as his two friends, Johnny Harris and Dick Thomas, had led him to practice with that novel weapon.

With a bound like an antelope he started toward the struggling men, swinging his lasso around his head as he ran. Pierre, believing that he had left Frank securely bound, and being too intent upon taking care of his new prisoner to look for enemies in his rear, heard not the sound of his approaching footsteps, nor did he dream of danger until the noose, which, but a few moments before, had been around Frank's neck, settled down over his own. Then he knew that his game was up. With a piercing cry of terror he sprang to his feet, and, with frantic haste, endeavored to throw off the lariat; but Frank was too quick for him.

"Aha!" he exclaimed, trying to imitate the tone in which the Ranchero had spoken that same word but a few moments before. "Aha! Now I am going to break one of two things - your spirit or your neck; I don't care which. One good turn deserves another, you know."

As Frank said this, he threw all his strength into his arms, and gave the lasso a vigorous jerk, which caused Pierre's heels to fly up, and his head to come in violent contact with the pavement of the court.

"Now, then, Uncle James," exclaimed Frank, "we've got him. No you don't!" he added, as the Ranchero made a desperate attempt to regain his feet; "come back here!" and he gave him a second jerk, which brought him to the ground again.

Frank was blessed with more than an ordinary share of muscle for a boy of his age; but he could not hope to compete successfully with a man of Pierre's size and experience, even though he held him at great disadvantage. The Ranchero, as active as a cat, thrashed about at an astonishing rate, and, before Frank knew what was going on, he had cut the lasso with his knife - an action which caused our hero, who was pulling back on the lariat with all his strength, to toss up his heels, and sit down upon the rough stones of the court, very suddenly, while Pierre, finding himself at liberty, jumped up, and ran for his life.

Mr. Winters had by this time regained his feet, and, catching up Frank's rifle, which lay beside him on the pavement, he took a flying shot at the robber just as he was running through the archway. Pierre's escape was a very narrow one; for the bullet went through the brim of his sombrero, and cut off a lock of his hair.

CHAPTER VI

THE MYSTERIES SOLVED

Pierre, finding himself uninjured by Mr. Winters's shot, suddenly became very courageous, and stopped to say a parting word to that gentleman.

"Try it again," said he, with a taunting laugh. "You are a poor shot for an old frontiersman! I will bid you good-by, now," he added, shaking his knife at Uncle James, "but you have not seen the last of me. You will have reason to remember" -

The Ranchero did not say what Mr. Winters would have reason to remember, for he happened to look toward the opposite side of the court, and saw something that brought from him an ejaculation of alarm, and caused him to turn and take to his heels. An instant afterward, a dark object bounded through the court, and, before the robber had taken half a dozen steps, Marmion sprang upon his back, and threw him to the ground.

"Hurrah!" shouted Frank. "You are not gone yet, it seems. You're caught now, easy enough; for that dog never lets go, if he once gets a good hold. Hang on to him, old fellow!"

But Marmion seemed to be utterly unable to manage the Ranchero. He had placed his fore-feet upon Pierre's breast, and appeared to be holding him by the throat; but the latter, with one blow of his arm, knocked him off, and, regaining his feet, fled through the grove with the speed of the wind - the piece of the lasso, which was still around his neck, streaming straight out behind him.

"Take him, Marmion!" yelled Frank, astonished to see his dog so easily defeated. "Take him! Hi! hi!"

The animal evidently did his best to obey; but there seemed to be something the matter with him. He ran as if he were dragging a heavy weight behind him, or as if his feet were tied together, and it was all he could do to keep up with the robber; and, when he tried to seize him, Pierre would shake him off without even slackening his pace.

Mr. Winters, in the meantime, had run to his horse - which, during the struggle, had stood perfectly still in the middle of the court - after his pistols; but, before he could get an opportunity to use them, both Pierre and the dog had disappeared among the trees. A moment afterward, a horse was heard going at full speed through the grove, indicating that the robber was leaving the ranch as fast as possible.

All this while, Frank has been almost overwhelmed with astonishment. The ease with which the desperado had vanquished his uncle and the strange behavior of the hitherto infallible Marmion, were things beyond his comprehension. He stood gazing, in stupid wonder, toward the trees among which Pierre had disappeared, while the sound of the horse's hoofs grew fainter and fainter, and finally died away altogether. Then he seemed to wake up, and to realize the fact that the Ranchero had made good his escape, in spite of all their efforts to capture him.

"Let's follow him, uncle!" he exclaimed, in an excited voice. "I can soon overtake him on Roderick."

"I could not ride a hundred yards to save my life!" replied Mr. Winters, seating himself on the porch, and resting his head on his hands. "Bring me some water, Frank."

These words alarmed the boy, who now, for the first time, saw that his uncle's face was deadly pale, and that his hair was matted with blood, which was trickling down over his collar.

"O, uncle!" cried Frank, in dismay.

"Don't be uneasy," said Mr. Winters, quietly. "Bring me some water."

Without stopping to make any inquiries, Frank ran into the kitchen and aroused the housekeeper, giving her a very hasty and disconnected account of what had happened, and then he hurried to the quarters to awaken Felix.

"Go to Fort Yuma for the doctor, at once!" shouted Frank, pounding loudly upon the door.

"What's up?" inquired Felix, from the inside.

"No matter what's up - go for the doctor! Take Roderick; he's the swiftest horse on the ranch. Uncle's badly wounded."

"Wounded!" repeated Felix, jerking open the door, and appearng upon the threshold, with a revolver in each hand. "Who did it? Where is he?"

"I can't stop to tell you who did it, or where he is. Hurry up, Felix, and don't stand there looking at me! We've just had the hardest kind of a fight with Pierre. Marmion was there, but he didn't do any good. He threw the villain down, and then wouldn't hold him. I've a good notion to shoot that dog if he ever comes back. Make haste, Felix! I can't stop to tell you any more."

But, after all, Frank did stop to tell a great deal more; and, by the time the Ranchero was dressed, he had given him a complete history of all that had happened in the house since sunset. Felix, astonished and enraged at the treachery of his companion, examined his pistols very carefully before he put them into his holsters, and Frank knew, by the expression in his eye, that if he should happen to meet Pierre, during his ride to the Fort, the latter would fall into dangerous hands.

As soon as Frank had seen Roderick saddled, he ran back to the house, and found Uncle James lying on a sofa, and the housekeeper engaged in dressing a long, ragged cut on the back of his head. Being weak from the loss of blood, he sank into a deep slumber before the operation was completed, and Frank, finding nothing to do, and being too nervous, after the exciting events of the evening, to keep still, went out to watch for the doctor, who, seeing that the Fort was sixteen miles from the ranch, could not reasonably be expected before daylight. For a long time he paced restlessly up and down the porch, his mind busy with the three questions that had so astonished and perplexed him: What had happened to bring his uncle home that night? How had he been so easily overpowered by Pierre? and, What was the matter with Marmion? The longer he pondered upon them, the more bewildered he became; and, finally dismissing them from his mind altogether, he went out to attend to his uncle's horse, which, all this while, had been running back and forth between the house and barn, now and then neighing shrilly, as if impatient at being so long neglected.

As Frank passed through the court, he picked up his rifle, which Mr. Winters had thrown down after taking that flying shot at Pierre. The stock felt damp in his grasp, and when he looked at his hand, he saw that it was red with blood.

"I understand one thing now, just as well as if I had stood here and witnessed it," said he, to himself. "When Pierre went out of my room, he ran in here to see who it was visiting the ranch at this late hour, and when he found that it was Uncle James, he thought he would get the safe key. He was too much of a coward to attack him openly, and so he slipped up and knocked him down with the butt of my rifle. That's what made the wound on uncle's head, and that's how it came that Pierre could hold him down with one hand. Didn't I know all the time that there was something up? Now, if Pierre had succeeded in getting the safe key, no doubt he would have renewed his attempts to make me tell where I had put the key of the office. Would I have been coward enough to do it? No, sir! I would have - Hallo!"

This exclamation was called forth by the sudden appearance of the dog, which crept slowly toward his master, looking altogether as if he had been guilty of something very mean.

"So you have got back, have you?" said Frank, sternly. "What do you mean by going off to hunt rabbits when you ought to stay at home? And what excuse have you to offer for allowing that robber to get up after you had pulled him down?"

Marmion stopped, and, laying his head close to the pavement, wagged his tail and whined piteously.

"I don't wonder that you feel ashamed of yourself," said his master. "Come here, you old coward."

The dog reluctantly obeyed, and, when he came nearer, another mystery was cleared up, and Frank knew why his favorite had behaved so strangely. One end of a rope was twisted about his jaws so tightly that he could scarcely move them, and the other, after being wound around his head and neck to keep the muzzle from slipping off, was fastened to both his fore feet, holding them so close together that it was a wonder that he could walk at all. Frank's anger vanished in an instant. He ran into his room after his knife, to release the dog from his bonds, and then he discovered that the animal had not come out of the fight unharmed. Two gaping wounds in his side bore evidence to the skill with which Pierre had handled his bowie.

At that moment, Frank felt a good deal as Llewellyn must have felt when he killed the hound which he imagined had devoured his child, but which had, in reality, defended him from the attacks of a wolf. He had scolded Marmion for his failure to hold the robber after he had thrown him down, and had been more than half inclined to give him a good beating; while the animal had, all the while, been doing his best, and, in spite of his wounds and bonds, had kept up the fight until Pierre mounted his horse and fled from the ranch.

The boy's first care, after he had removed the rope, was to bandage the wounds as well as he could, and to lead the dog to a comfortable bed on the porch, where he left him to await the arrival of the doctor; for Frank resolved that, as Marmion had received his injuries during the performance of his duty, he should have the very best of care.

Frank never closed his eyes that night. He passed the hours in pacing up and down the porch watching for the Ranchero, who made his appearance shortly after daylight, accompanied by the doctor. Mr. Winters's wound, although very painful, was not a dangerous one, and after it had been dressed by the skillful hands of the surgeon, he felt well enough to enter into conversation with those around him.

"Now," said Frank, who had been impatiently awaiting an opportunity to talk to his uncle, "I'd like to know what brought you back here last night?"

"I came after the twelve thousand dollars," replied Mr. Winters. "When I arrived in the city, I learned that Mr. Brown had left there early in the morning to pay us a visit, taking with him the money he owed me. I wanted to use it immediately, and as I did not know what might happen if it should become known that there was so much money in the house, and no one here to take care of it, I came home; but I should have lost the money after all, if it hadn't been for you, Frank, and I might have lost my life with it; for I believe the villain was in earnest."

"I am quite sure he was," said Frank, feeling of his neck, which still bore the marks of the lasso in the shape of a bright red streak. "If you had stayed away five minutes longer, I should have been hanged. O, it's a fact!" he added, earnestly, noticing that the doctor looked at him incredulously. "I came very near dancing on nothing, now I tell you; and if you only knew all that has happened in this house since dark , youwouldn't say that there was no one here to take care of that money. But, uncle, how came you by that wound?"

"Pierre gave it to me," was the reply. "He slipped up behind me when I was dismounting, and struck me with something. But what did he do to you?"

"He pulled me up by the neck with my own lasso," replied Frank; "that's what he did to me."

"The scoundrel!" exclaimed the doctor. "Tell us all about it."

Thus encouraged, Frank began and related his story, to which his auditors listened with breathless attention. He told what he had done with the twelve thousand dollars, where he had hidden the keys, how he had detected Pierre watching him through the window, and how the Ranchero had told him that Marmion was off hunting rabbits, when he was lying bound and muzzled in some out-of-the-way place. Then he explained how the robber had overpowered him while he was reading, how he had searched his pockets for the keys, and pulled him up by the neck because he refused to tell where he had hidden them, and how he was on the very point of hanging him in earnest when the arrival of Uncle James alarmed him. Mr. Winters was astonished, and so was the doctor, who patted Frank on the head, and said:

"You're a chip of the old block. And did you not tell him where you had put the key?"

"No, sir;" was the answer. "He choked me pretty hard, though, and my throat feels funny yet."

The boy having finished his story, Mr. Winters took it up where he left off, and told the doctor how Frank had rescued him from the robber, and how hard he had worked to effect his capture, and all who heard it declared that he was a hero.

CHAPTER VII

FRANK MEETS A HIGHWAYMAN

Frank passed the next day in making up for the sleep he had lost the night before. About three o'clock in the afternoon he arose refreshed, and visited his uncle, whom he found fast asleep. Now that Archie was gone, the old house was quiet and lonesome - too much so, indeed, to suit Frank, who, after trying in vain to find some way to amuse himself until supper time, saddled Roderick, and set out for a short gallop over the prairie. As he was about to mount his horse, Marmion came out of the court, and frisked about his master as lively as ever, apparently none the worse for the ugly-looking wounds he had received during his encounter with the robber.

"Go home, sir," said Frank. "Don't you know that you are under the doctor's care?"

If Marmion did know it, he didn't bother his head about it. He had a will of his own; and having always been permitted to accompany his master wherever he went, he did not feel disposed to remain behind. Instead of obeying the command to go home, he ran on before, and Frank made no further attempts to drive him back.

Frank, having by this time become well acquainted with the country for twenty miles around his uncle's rancho, knew where he wanted to go, and about an hour after he left home, he was stretched at full length beside a spring among the mountains, where he and his friends often camped to eat their dinner during their hunting expeditions. Roderick stood close by, lazily cropping the grass, but Marmion was not in sight. The last time his master saw him, he was trying to gnaw his way into a hollow log where a rabbit had taken refuge.

Frank lay beside the spring until his increasing hunger reminded him that it was nearly supper time, and then he mounted his horse, and started for home. Roderick being permitted to choose his own gait, walked slowly along a narrow bridle-path that led out of the mountains, and Frank sat in his saddle with both hands in his pockets, his sombrero pulled down over his eyes, and his thoughts wandering away to the ends of the earth. He had ridden in this way about half a mile, when he was suddenly aroused from his meditations by a commotion in the bushes at his side, and the next moment a man sprang in front of the horse, and seized him by the bridle.

"Pierre Costello!" exclaimed Frank, as soon as he had somewhat recovered from his astonishment.

"Ay, it's Pierre, and no mistake," returned the Ranchero, with a triumphant smile. "You thought I had left the country, didn't you?"

"I was in hopes you had; but I see you are still on hand, like a bad dollar-bill."

"We are well met," continued Pierre. "I have been waiting for an opportunity to thank you for the very friendly manner in which you treated me last night."

"You need not have put yourself to any trouble about it. You are under no obligations to me. As I am in something of a hurry, I will now bid you good-by."

"Not if I know myself, and I think I do," said Pierre, with a laugh. "You are just as impudent as ever. Climb down off that horse."

Frank's actions indicated that he did not think it best to obey this order. He sat perfectly still in his saddle, looking at Pierre, and wondering what he should do. He could show no weapon to intimidate the robber, for he was entirely unarmed, not having brought even his lasso or clasp-knife with him; while Pierre held in his hand, ready for instant use, the bowie that had rendered him such good service during the fight in the court. At first Frank entertained the bold idea of riding over the Ranchero. Roderick was as quick as a flash in his movements, and one touch of the spurs, if his rider could take Pierre off his guard, would cause the horse to jerk the bridle from his grasp, and before the robber could recover himself, Frank would be out of danger. But Pierre had anticipated this movement, and he was too well acquainted with his prisoner to relax his vigilance for an instant. More than that, he held both the reins under Roderick's jaw with a firm grasp, and stood in such a position that he could control the movements of both the horse and his rider.

A moment's reflection having satisfied Frank that his idea of running over Pierre could not be carried out, he began to look around for his dog. But Marmion had not yet come up, and Frank was compelled to acknowledge to himself that he was as completely in the villain's power as he had been when Pierre had the lasso around his neck.

"Get down off that horse, I say," commanded the Ranchero.

"So you have turned highwayman, have you?" said Frank, without moving. "Do you find it a more pleasant and profitable business than herding cattle?"

"Are you going to get off that horse?" asked the robber, impatiently.

"What's the use? You will not find a red cent in my pockets."

"I suppose not; but if I take you with me, I'll soon find out how many yellow boys your uncle carries in his pockets."

"If you take me with you!" repeated Frank. "What do you mean?"

"I mean just this: I shall find it exceedingly lonesome living here in the mountains by myself, and I don't know of any one in the world I had rather have for a companion than yourself."

"Humph!" exclaimed Frank; "that's a nice idea. I won't go."

"Of course," continued the Ranchero, not heeding the interruption, "when you fail to make your appearance at home for three or four days, your uncle will think he has seen the last of you. He will believe that you have been clawed up by grizzlies, or that you have tumbled into some of these gullies. He will raise a hue and cry, search high and low for you, offer rewards, and all that; and, while the fuss is going on, and people are wondering what in the world could have become of you, you will be safe and sound, and living like a gentleman, with me, on the fat of the land."

"But, Pierre," said Frank, now beginning to be really frightened, "I don't want to live with you on the fat of the land, and I won't do it. Let go that bridle."

The Ranchero, as before, paid no attention to the interruption. He seemed to delight in tormenting his prisoner.

"After you have been with me about six months," he went on, "and your friends have given up all hope of ever seeing you again, I'll send a note to Mr. Winters, stating that you are alive and well, and that, if he will give me twenty thousand dollars in gold, I will return you to him in good order, right side up with care. If I find that we can get along pretty well together, I may conclude to keep you a year; for the longer you remain away from your uncle, the more he will want to see you, and the bigger will be the pile he will give to have you brought back. What is your opinion of that plan? Don't you think it a capital way to raise the wind?"

Frank listened to this speech in utter bewilderment. Cruel and reckless as he knew Pierre to be, he had never for a moment imagined that he could be guilty of such an enormous crime as this. He did not know what reply to make - there was nothing he could say or do. Entreaties and resistance were alike useless.

"Well, what are you thinking about?" inquired the Ranchero.

"I was wondering if a greater villain than yourself ever lived," replied Frank.

"We will talk about that as we go along," said Pierre. "Get off that horse, now; I am going to send him home."

Frank, seeing no way of escape, was about to obey this order, when the truant, Marmion, came in sight, trotting leisurely up the path, carrying in his mouth the rabbit, which he had succeeded in gnawing out of the log. He stopped short on discovering Pierre, dropped his game, and gathered himself for a spring.

"Take him, Marmion!" yelled Frank, as he straightened himself up in his saddle. "If it is all the same to you, Mr. Pierre, I'll not go to the mountains this evening."

The Ranchero did not wait to receive the dog. He was an arrant coward, and, more than that, he stood as much in fear of Marmion as if he had been a bear or panther. Uttering a cry of terror, he dropped the bridle, and, with one bound, disappeared in the bushes. Marmion followed close at his heels, encouraged by terrific yells from his master, who, now that his dog was neither bound nor muzzled, looked upon the capture of the robber as a thing beyond a doubt. There was a loud crashing and snapping in the bushes, as the pursuer and pursued sped on their way, and presently another loud yell of terror, mingled with an angry growl, told Frank that the dog had come up with Pierre.

"He is caught at last," thought our hero; "how shall I get him home? that's the question. How desperately he fights," he added, as the commotion in the bushes increased, and the yells and growls grew louder. "But he'll find it's no use, for he can't whip that dog, if he has got a knife. Now, I ought to have a rope. I'll ride up the path, and see if I can find Pierre's horse; and, if I can, I'll take his lasso and tie the rascal hand and foot."

Frank galloped up the path a short distance, but could see nothing of the horse. The Ranchero had, doubtless, left him in the bushes, and Frank was about to dismount and go in search of him, when, to his utter astonishment, he saw Pierre coming toward him. His face was badly scratched; his jacket and shirt had disappeared altogether; his breast and arms were covered with blood, and so was his knife, which he still held in his hand. But, where was Marmion, that he was not following up his enemy? The answer was plain. The dog had been worsted in his encounter with the robber, and Frank was left to fight his battles alone. He thought no more of taking Pierre a prisoner to the rancho. All he cared for now was to escape.

"Well, now, it was good of you not to run away when you had the chance," said the Ranchero, who appeared to be quite as much surprised at seeing Frank as the latter had been at seeing him.

"If I had thought that you could get away from that dog, I should have been a mile from here by this time," replied Frank. "I was looking for your horse, and, if I had found him, I should have gone to Marmion's assistance."

"Well, he needed you bad enough," said Pierre, with a laugh. "I have fixed him this time."

"You have!" cried Frank, his worst suspicions confirmed. "Is Marmion dead?"

"Dead as a door-nail. Now we must be off; we have wasted too much time already."

If the Ranchero supposed that Frank would allow himself to be captured a second time, he was sadly mistaken. The boy was free, and he determined to remain so.

"Pierre," said he, filled with rage at the words of the robber, "I may have a chance to square accounts with you some day, and if I do I'll remember that you killed my dog."

"Come, now, no nonsense," said the Ranchero, gruffly. "You are my prisoner, you know."

"I think not. Stand where you are; don't come a step nearer."

While this conversation was going on, Pierre had been walking slowly up the path, and, as Frank ceased speaking, he made a sudden rush, intending to seize Roderick by the bridle. But his rider was on the alert. Gathering his reins firmly in his hands, he dashed his spurs into the flanks of his horse, which sprang forward like an arrow from a bow, and thundered down the path toward Pierre, who turned pale with terror.

"Out of the way, you villain, or I'll ride you down," shouted Frank.

This was very evident to the Ranchero, who, seizing upon the only chance for escape offered him, plunged head-foremost into the bushes. He barely missed being run down, for Roderick flew by before he was fairly out of the path, and, by the time he had recovered his feet, Frank was out of sight.

When Frank reached home, he shed a great many tears over Marmion's untimely death; but, as it happened, it was grief wasted. One morning, about a week after his adventure with the highwayman, while Frank and Archie were out for their morning's ride, a sorry-looking object crawled into the court, and thence into the office, where Mr. Winters was busy at his desk. "Mad dog!" shouted the gentleman, when he discovered the intruder; and, springing to his feet, he lifted his chair over his head, and was in the very act of extinguishing the last spark of life left in the poor brute, when the sight of a collar he wore around his neck arrested his hand. It was no wonder that Uncle James had not recognized the animal, for he looked very unlike the lively, well-conditioned dog which Frank was wont to regard as the apple of his eye. But, nevertheless, it was Marmion, or, rather, all that was left of him. He had been severely wounded, and was nearly starved; but he received the best of care, and it was not long before he was as savage and full of fight as ever. Although he had failed to capture the robber, he had rendered his master a most important service, and no one ever heard him find fault with Marmion after that.

Frank's reputation was by this time firmly established, and he was the lion of the settlement. Dick Lewis was prouder than ever of him. Of course, he called him a "keerless feller," and read him several long lectures, illustrating them by incidents drawn from his own experience. He related the story of Frank's adventures with the robber every time he could induce any one to listen to it, and ever afterward called him "the boy that fit that ar' Greaser." Old Bob Kelly beamed benevolently upon him every time they met, and more than once told his companion that the "youngster would make an amazin' trapper;" and that, in Dick's estimation, was a compliment worth all the rest.

Meanwhile, the country had been made exceedingly unsafe for Pierre Costello. The neighbors had turned out in force, every nook and corner of the mountains for miles around had been searched, and a large reward offered for the robber's apprehension; but it was all in vain. Nothing more had been heard of Pierre, and Frank hoped that he had seen him for the last time. Fate, however, had decreed that he was to have other adventures with the highwayman.

CHAPTER VIII

COLONEL ARTHUR VANE

We left Frank and Archie standing on the porch, watching the wild steer which was being led toward the cow-pen. As soon as they had got over their excitement, they remembered that they had saddled their horses for the purpose of riding over to visit their nearest neighbor, Johnny Harris, one of the boys whose daring horsemanship, and skill with the lasso, had so excited their admiration. Johnny lived four miles distant; but he and the cousins were together almost all the time. If Johnny was not at their house, Frank and Archie were at his; and when you saw one of the three, it was a sure sign that the others were not a great way off. Dick Thomas, of whom mention has been made, had been one of the party; but he was now on a visit to San Francisco and would not return until winter.

Had Frank and his cousin, while at home, been compelled to ride or walk four miles in search of a playmate, they might have been disposed to grumble over what they would have considered a very hard lot in life; but they had learned to think nothing of it. There were their horses always ready and willing, and half an hour's gallop over the prairie in the cool of the morning, or evening, was not looked upon as any thing very disagreeable. On this particular morning, Roderick and Marmion were impatient to exhibit their mettle; and even Sleepy Sam lifted his head and pawed the ground when Archie placed his foot in the stirrup. Scarcely waiting for their riders to become firmly seated in their saddles, the horses started down the road at a rattling pace, and the dog dashed through the bushes and grass on each side, driving the rabbits from their covers, and creating great consternation among flocks of quails and prairie-chickens, which flew up at his approach.

The farther the boys went, the faster they went; for Roderick and Sleepy Sam, warming at their work, and encouraged, perhaps, by some slight touches from their riders' spurs, increased their speed until they fairly flew over the ground; and Marmion, unwilling to remain behind, left the quails and rabbits to rest in security for that morning at least, and ran along beside his master, now and then looking up into his face, and uttering a little yelp, as if he were trying to tell how well he enjoyed the sport.

"Now, isn't this glorious?" exclaimed Archie, pulling off his sombrero, and holding open his jacket, to catch every breath of the fresh morning air. "Let's go faster. Yip! yip!"

The horses understood that yell. They had heard it before; and, knowing that it meant a race, they set off at the top of their speed. But the race was not a long one; for the old buffalo hunter, fast as he was, soon fell behind. The gray flew over the ground, as swiftly as a bird on the wing, and, after allowing him a free rein for a short distance, to show Archie how badly he could beat him, Frank stopped, and waited for him to come up.

The four miles were quickly accomplished, and, presently, the boys drew up at the door of Mr. Harris's farm-house, where they found Johnny waiting to receive them.

"How are you, strangers?" cried Johnny. "Get down and make those posts fast to your horses, and come in."

This was the way travelers were welcomed in that country, where every house was a hotel, and every farmer ready, at all times, to feed and shelter a stranger.

"How is the rifle-shot, this morning?" continued Johnny, as he shook hands with the boys; "and what news has the champion horseman to communicate?"

"I didn't claim to be the champion horseman," said Archie, quickly. "I am not conceited enough to believe that I can beat you riding wild horses, but I'll tell you what I can do, Johnny. In a fair race from here to the mountains, I can leave you a quarter of a mile behind."

"Well, come in, and wait till I saddle my horse, and we'll see about that," said Johnny. "Until you came here, I could beat any boy in the settlement. I give in to Frank, but I can show that ugly old buffalo hunter of yours a pretty pair of heels. Boys!" he added, suddenly, "my day's fun is all knocked in the head. See there!"

The cousins looked in the direction indicated, and saw a horseman approaching at a rapid gallop. He was mounted on a large iron-gray, which looked enough like Roderick to have been his brother, sat as straight as an arrow in his saddle, and managed his fiery charger with an ease and dexterity that showed him to be an accomplished rider.

"That's *Colonel* Arthur Vane - a neighbor with whom you are not yet acquainted," said Johnny, with strong emphasis on the word colonel. "He is from Kentucky. His father came to this country about six months since, and bought the rancho adjoining your uncle's. Arthur remained here long enough for Dick and me to become as well acquainted with him as we cared to be, and then went back to Kentucky to visit his friends. He returned a few days ago, and now we may make up our minds to have him for a companion."

"What sort of a fellow is he, Johnny?" asked Frank.

"I don't admire him," replied Johnny, who, like Archie, never hesitated to speak his mind very freely. "From what I have seen of him, I should say that he is not a boy who is calculated to make friends. He talks and brags too much. He tries to use big words in conversation, and criticises every one around him most unmercifully. He is one of those knowing fellows; but, after you have exchanged a few words with him, you will find that he doesn't know so very much after all. He has been all over the world, if we are to believe what he says, and has been the hero of adventures that throw your encounter with Pierre Costello into the shade. He carries no less than seven bullets in his body."

"Seven bullets!" echoed Archie. "Why, I should think they would kill him."

"So they would, most likely, if he only had them in him," replied Johnny. "He is a famous hunter and trapper, owns two splendid horses, a pack of hounds, three or four fine guns, and makes himself hot and happy in a suit of buckskin. If it were not for his smooth face and dandy airs, one would take him for some old mountain man. He gave Dick and me a short history of his life - which he will be sure to repeat for your benefit - and was foolish enough to believe that we were as green as two pumpkins because we had never been in the States, and that we would swallow any thing. But, if we have always lived in a wilderness, we have not neglected our books, and we are well enough posted to know that Arthur makes great mistakes sometimes."

"But why is your day's fun all knocked in the head?" asked Archie.

"Because I can't enjoy myself when Arthur is around. I am always afraid that I shall do or say something that he won't like. Every time I look at him, I am reminded of Byron's Corsair, who, you know, was

> ' - the mildest mannered man
> That ever scuttled ship or cut a throat.'

I don't mean to say that Arthur would cut any body's throat, but I do say that if he should happen to get angry at any of us, we shall wish him safe in Kentucky, where he belongs. I can't very well avoid introducing him, but, after what I have said, you will understand that I do not indorse him."

The conversation was brought to a close by the near approach of Arthur Vane, who presently dashed up to the porch, and dismounted. Frank and Archie made a rapid examination of the new-comer. He was dressed in a full suit of buckskin - hunting-shirt, leggins, and moccasins, the latter ornamented with bright-colored beads - which set off his tall, slender, well-knit frame to good advantage. He evidently possessed a fair share of muscle and agility, and that, according to Archie's way of thinking, was a great recommendation. He little dreamed that his own pluck, strength, and endurance would one day be severely tested by that boy in buckskin.

Arthur's weapons were objects of no less curiosity to the cousins than his dress. Instead of the short, light rifle in which the boys of that country took so much delight, and which was so handy to be used on horseback, he carried a double-barrel shot-gun as long as himself, elaborately ornamented, and the boys judged, from the way he handled it, that it must be very heavy. From his belt protruded the buckhorn handle of a sheath-knife, and the bright, polished head of an Indian tomahawk. The lasso was nowhere to be seen.

When the boys had noted these points, they glanced at the face of the new-comer. It was a handsome face, and might have made a favorable impression on them, had it not been for the haughty glances which its owner directed toward them as he rode up.

"He looks at us as though he thought we had no business here," whispered Archie, as Johnny went down the steps to receive the visitor.

"A second Charley Morgan," replied his cousin.

"If he is blessed with Morgan's amiable disposition," returned Archie, "we'll see fun before we are done with him."

"Frank Nelson," said Johnny, leading his visitor upon the porch, "this is our new neighbor, Arthur Vane."

"Colonel of the Second Kentucky Cavalry during the Florida war, and, for a short time captain of the scouts attached to the head-quarters of the general commanding the department of the plains," said Arthur, in dignified tones, drawing himself up to his full height, and looking at Frank as if to ask, What do you think of me, anyhow?

"How do you do?" said Frank, accepting Vane's proffered hand. He did not say that he was glad to see him, or happy to make his acquaintance, for he wasn't.

"Archie Winters, Colonel Vane," continued Johnny, "formerly commander of the Second Kentucky - ahem!"

Johnny was going on to repeat Arthur's pompous speech, when he saw Archie biting his lip, and knew that it was time for him to stop.

"How are you, Colonel?" said Archie, as sober as a judge.

"I can not complain of my health," replied Arthur, still holding Frank's hand with his right, while he extended his left to Archie, in much the same manner that a monarch might have given his hand to a kneeling subject. "The musket-ball that Osceola sent through my shoulder sometimes troubles me a little; but I am so accustomed to wounds that I scarcely mind it."

"How do you like California," inquired Frank, thinking that he ought to say something.

"O, I like the country well enough; but belonging, as I do, to one of the oldest and wealthiest families of the State of

Kentucky, I can find no congenial society among these backwoodsmen."

Frank had no reply to make to this declaration. That one remark had revealed as much of the character of Arthur Vane as he cared to become acquainted with. The latter evidently looked upon himself as something better than the common herd of mankind, and Frank wondered why he did not stay at home, if he could find no pleasure in the society of the boys of that country.

"I have heard of you," continued Arthur, loftily; "and I understand that you are looked upon as a hero in this settlement."

"I do not claim the honor," modestly replied Frank.

"I have always observed," the visitor went on to say, "that the ideas which ignorant people entertain concerning heroes are ludicrous in the extreme. Now, I have met with more adventures than generally fall to the lot of mortals; but, being a modest young man, I have never allowed any one to apply that name to me. I have been in battles - desperate battles. I have seen the cheek of the bravest blanched with terror; but I never flinched. Twice have I been a prisoner in the hands of the Indians, and once I was bound to the stake. I have whipped a grizzly bear in a fair fight, with no weapon but my knife, and I can show seven honorable scars, made by as many bullets, which I carry in my body to-day."

Here Arthur stopped to take breath, and looked at his auditors as if waiting for applause. Frank and Archie had nothing to say, but Johnny observed:

"You have seen some rough times for one of your age."

"Rough!" repeated Arthur, with evident disgust. "Don't use such words - they are so vulgar. Thrilling, or exciting, would sound much better."

"I stand corrected," remarked Johnny, very gravely, while Archie coughed, and Frank turned away his head to conceal his laughter.

"I can not begin to convey to you even a slight idea of what I have endured," said Arthur, as if nothing had happened. "It is true that I am young in years, but I am old in experience. I have known every variety of danger incident to a reckless and roving life. I have skirmished with Arabs on the burning sands of Patagonia; have hunted the ferocious polar bear amid the icebergs of India; have followed lions and tigers through the jungles and forests of Europe; have risked my life in four different battles with the Algerines, and, on one occasion, was captured by those murderous villains. If adventures make the hero, I can certainly lay claim to that honor as well as anybody."

As the visitor ceased speaking, he looked suspiciously at the three boys before him, two of whom seemed to be strangely affected by the recital of his thrilling adventures. Frank had grown very red in the face, while Johnny was holding his handkerchief over his mouth, trying to restrain a violent fit of coughing with which he had suddenly been seized. Archie was the only one who could keep a straight face. He stood with his hands behind his back, his feet spread out, his sombrero pushed as far back on his head as he could get it, looking intently at Arthur, as if he were very much interested in what he was saying. He came to the relief of the others, however, by observing:

"If I had seen all those countries you speak of, Vane, I should be proud of it. No one delights more in truthful stories of adventure than I do, and, if you have no objection, we will sit down here and talk, while Johnny saddles his horse. We are going over to visit old Captain Porter. You will go with us, of course?"

"Certainly. I have often heard of Captain Porter, and I shall be pleased to make his acquaintance. He and I can talk over our adventures, and you can listen, and you will, no doubt, learn something."

Johnny, knowing that Frank wanted some excuse to get away where he could enjoy a hearty laugh, asked him to assist in catching his horse; and, together, they went toward the barn, leaving Archie behind to listen to Arthur's stories.

CHAPTER IX

AN OLD BOY

By the exercise of wonderful self-control, Frank and Johnny succeeded in restraining their risibilities until they reached the barn, and then one leaned against the door-post, while the other seated himself upon the floor, both holding their sides, and giving vent to peals of uproarious laughter.

"O dear!" exclaimed Frank, "I shall never dare look that fellow in the face again. 'Icebergs of India!' 'Burning sands of Patagonia!' How my jaws ache!"

"I wonder what part of Europe he visited to find his lions and tigers?" said Johnny. "And how do you suppose he escaped from the Indians when they had him bound to the stake? We must ask him about that."

"How old is he?" inquired Frank.

"He says he is sixteen."

"Well, he is older than that, if he risked his life in battles with the Algerians; for, if my memory serves me, Decatur settled our accounts with those gentlemen in the year 1815. That would make our new friend old enough to be a grandfather. He holds his age well, doesn't he?"

Then the two boys looked up at the rafters, and laughed louder than ever.

"I remember of hearing old Captain Porter say," observed Johnny, as soon as he could speak, "that the strongest and most active man that ever lived could not whip a grizzly in a fair fight; and that the bravest hunter would take to his heels if he found himself in close quarters with one of those animals, and would not think he was guilty of cowardice, either."

"And what I have seen with my own eyes confirms it," said Frank. "While we were camped at the Old Bear's Hole, Dick Lewis got into a fight with a grizzly, and, although it didn't last more than half a minute, he was so badly cut up that his own mother wouldn't have recognized him. Dick is a giant in strength, and as quick as a cat in his movements, and if he can't whip a grizzly, I am sure that Arthur Vane can't."

"Humph!" said Johnny, "he never saw a grizzly. I never did either, and there are plenty of them in this country. Arthur had better be careful how he talks in Captain Porter's hearing. The rough old fellow will see through him in an instant, and he may not be as careful of his feelings as we have been."

Johnny, having by this time saddled his horse, he and Frank returned to the house, where they found Archie deeply interested in one of Arthur's stories. "That is high up, I should think," they heard the former say.

"Yes, higher than the tops of these trees," replied Arthur. "I was relating some of the incidents of one of my voyages at sea," he continued, addressing himself to Frank. "I was telling Archie how I used to stand on the very top of the mast and look out for whales."

"Which mast?" asked Frank.

"Why, the middle mast, of course. What's the matter with you?" he added, turning suddenly upon Archie, who seemed to be on the point of strangling.

"Nothing," was the reply, "only something got stuck in my throat."

Arthur had taken up a dangerous subject when he began to talk about nautical matters; for they were something in which Frank and his cousin had always been interested, and were well posted. Archie lived in a sea-port town, and, although he had never been a sailor, he knew the names of all the ropes, and could talk as "salt" as any old tar. He knew, and so did Frank, that what Arthur had called the "middle mast," was known on shipboard as the mainmast. They knew that the "very top" of the mainmast was called the main truck; and that the look-outs were not generally stationed so high up in the world.

"We can talk as we ride along," said Johnny. "We have ten miles to go, and we ought to reach the captain's by twelve o'clock. The old fellow tells a capital story over his after-dinner pipe."

The boys mounted their horses, and, led by Johnny, galloped off in the direction of the old fur-trader's ranch. They rode in silence for a few minutes, and then Archie said:

"If you wouldn't think me too inquisitive, Arthur, I'd like to know at what age you began your travels?"

"At the age of eleven," was the prompt reply, "I was a midshipman in the navy, and made my first voyage under the gallant Decatur. I spent four years at sea with him, and during that time I had those terrible fights with the Algerines, of which I have before spoken. In the last battle, I was captured, and compelled to walk the plank."

"What do you mean by that?" asked Johnny, who had never devoted any of his time to yellow-covered literature.

"Why, you must know that the inhabitants of Algiers, and the adjacent countries, were, at one time, nothing but pirates. When they captured a vessel, their first hard work, after taking care of the valuable part of the cargo, was to dispose of their prisoners. It was too much trouble to set them ashore, so they balanced a plank out of one of the gangways - one end being out over the water, and the other on board the ship. The pirates placed their feet on the end inboard, to hold it in its place, and then ordered their prisoners, one at a time, to walk out on the plank. Of course, they were compelled to obey; and, when they got out to the end of the plank over the water, the pirates lifted up their feet, and down went the prisoners; and they generally found their way to the bottom in a hurry. I escaped by swimming. I was in the water twenty-four hours, and was picked up by a vessel bound to New York."

"I suppose you had a life-preserver," said Johnny.

"No, sir. I had nothing to depend upon but my own exertions."

"You must be some relation to a duck," said Archie, speaking before he thought.

"I suppose you mean to convey the idea that I am an excellent swimmer," said Arthur, turning around in his saddle, and looking sharply at Archie.

"Yes; that's what I intended to say," replied Archie, demurely.

"The vessel landed me in New York," continued Arthur, "and I went home; and, having become tired of wandering about, and our troubles with Algiers being settled, I led the quiet life of a student until the Florida war broke out, and then I enlisted in the army."

"Now, then," thought Archie, who had been paying strict attention to all Arthur said, "I have got a basis for a calculation, and I am going to find out how old this new friend of ours is. War was declared against Algeria (not Algiers) in March, 1815; and on the 30th day of June, in the same year, the Dey cried for quarter, and signed a treaty of peace. If

Arthur began his wanderings at eleven, and spent four years with Decatur, he must have been fifteen years old when the war closed. After that, he led the quiet life of a student until the Florida war broke out. That commenced in 1835; so Arthur must have spent just twenty years at school. By the way, it's a great pity that he didn't devote a portion of his time to geography and natural history, for then he would have known that there are no icebergs and polar bears in India, or Arabs and burning sands in Patagonia, or wild lions and tigers in Europe. If he spent twenty years at school, and was fifteen years old when he had those terrible battles with the Algerians, he must have been thirty-five years old when the Florida war broke out."

"Did you go through the war?" Johnny asked.

"I did."

"How long did it last?" inquired Frank, "and what was the cause of it?"

"It continued nearly two years, and was brought about by the hatred the Choctaws cherished toward the white people."

"Three mistakes there," thought Archie. "The war lasted seven years, and cost our Government forty millions of dollars. The Choctaws had nothing to do with it. It was the Seminoles and Creeks - principally the former. The immediate cause of the trouble was the attempt on the part of the Government to remove those tribes to the country west of the Mississippi. They didn't want to go, and they were determined they wouldn't; and, consequently, they got themselves decently whipped. If Arthur was thirty-five years of age when he went into the war, and spent two years in it, he was thirty-seven when he came out."

"After the war closed," continued Arthur, "I went to Patagonia, and there I spent five years."

"Thirty-seven and five are forty-two," said Archie, to himself.

"I had a great many thrilling adventures in Patagonia. The country is one immense desert, and being directly under the equator, it is - if you will for once allow me to use a slang expression - as hot as a frying-pan. The Arabs are hostile, and are more troublesome than ever the Indians were on the plains. From Patagonia I went to Europe, and there I spent six years in hunting lions and tigers."

"Forty-eight," thought Archie; "and Patagonia isn't under the equator, either."

"That must have been exciting," said Frank, while Johnny looked over his shoulder, and grinned at Archie.

"It was indeed exciting, and dangerous, too. It takes a man with nerves of iron to stand perfectly still, and let a roaring lion walk up within ten paces of him, before he puts a bullet through his head."

"Could you do it?"

"Could I? I have done it more than once. If one of those ferocious animals were here now, I would give you a specimen of my shooting, which is an accomplishment in which I can not be beaten. I expect that you would be so badly frightened that you would desert me, and leave me to fight him alone."

"Wouldn't you run?"

"Not an inch."

"Would you fire that blunderbuss at him?" asked Johnny.

"Blunderbuss?" repeated Arthur.

"That shot-gun, I mean."

"Certainly I would. You see I have the nerve to do it. From Europe I went to India, and there I risked my life for six years more among the polar bears."

"Forty-eight and six are fifty-four," soliloquized Archie.

"After that I went to the plains, where I remained three years; and when the governor wrote to me that he was about to remove from Kentucky, I resigned my commission as captain of scouts, and here I am. I must confess that I am sorry enough for it; for I never saw a duller country than California. There's no society here, no excitement - nothing to stir up a fellow's blood."

"Fifty-four and three are fifty-seven," said Archie.

Arthur had evidently finished the history of his exploits, for he had nothing more to say just then. Archie, after waiting a few minutes for him to resume his narrative, pulled his sombrero down over his eyes, and thrust his hands into his pockets - two movements he always executed when he wished to concentrate his mind upon any thing - and began to ponder upon what he had just heard.

"Vane," said he, suddenly, an idea striking him, "who commanded your vessel when you were captured?"

Arthur knitted his brows, and looked down at the horn of his saddle, as if thinking intently, and finally said: "Why, it was Mr. - , Mr. - ; I declare, I have forgotten his name."

Archie again relapsed into silence.

"We had two wars with those pirates," thought he. "The first was with Tripoli; but as that happened in 1805, Arthur, of course, could not have taken part in it, for he made his first voyage at sea in 1815. We lost but one vessel, and that was captured in 1803 - two years before war with Tripoli was declared. It was the frigate Philadelphia, and she wasn't whipped, either, but was run aground while pursuing a piratical vessel. She was commanded by Captain Bainbridge, who surrendered himself and crew. They were not compelled to 'walk the plank,' however, but were reduced to a horrible captivity, and treated worse than dogs. The Tripolitans never got a chance to use the Philadelphia against us, for Decatur - who was at that time a lieutenant serving under Commodore Preble, who commanded our navy in those waters - boarded her one night with twenty men while she was lying in the harbor, swept the deck of more than double that number of pirates, burned the vessel under their very noses, and returned to his ship with only one man wounded. I never did care much for history, but a fellow finds a great deal of satisfaction sometimes in knowing a little about it."

Archie had at first been highly amused by what Arthur had to say; but now, that the novelty had somewhat worn off, he began to wonder how it was possible for a boy to look another in the face and tell such improbable stories. If Arthur was not ashamed of himself Archie was heartily ashamed for him, and he was more than half inclined to put spurs to Sleepy Sam and start for home. He was not fond of such company.

Arthur Vane is not an imaginary character. There are a great many like him in the world, boys, and men, too, who endeavor to make amends for the absence of real merit by recounting just such impossible exploits. The result, however, is always the exact reverse of what they wish it to be. Instead of impressing their auditors with a sense of their great importance, they only succeed in awakening in their minds feelings of pity and contempt.

After Arthur had finished the history of his life, he rode along whistling snatches of the "Hunter's Chorus," happy in the belief that his reputation was established. Well, it was established, but how? Archie thought: "Brag is a splendid dog, but Holdfast is better. Perhaps we may have a chance to test the courage of this mighty man of valor."

Johnny soliloquized: "Does this fellow imagine that we are green enough to believe that he would stand and let a lion walk up within ten paces of him? Hump! a good-sized rabbit would scare him to death."

Frank, who had taken but little part in the conversation, told himself that he had never become acquainted with a boy as deserving of pity as was Arthur Vane. He was not a desirable companion, and Frank hoped that he would not often be thrown into his society.

For a long time the boys rode in silence, keeping their horses in an easy gallop, and presently they entered the woods that fringed the base of the mountains, through which ran a bridle-path that led toward the old fur-trader's ranch. Two young hounds belonging to Johnny led the way, Johnny came next, and Frank and Archie brought up the rear. They had ridden in this order for a short distance, when the singular movements of the hounds attracted their attention, and caused them to draw rein. The dogs stood in the path, snuffing the air, and gazing intently at the bushes in advance of them, and then, suddenly uttering a dismal howl, they ran back to the boys, and took refuge behind them. At the same instant, the horse on which Johnny was mounted arose on his hind feet, turned square around, and, in spite of all the efforts of his rider to stop him, dashed by the others, and went down the path at the top of his speed.

"Good-by, fellows," shouted Johnny; "and look out for yourselves, for there is" -

What else Johnny said the boys could not understand, for the clatter of his horse's hoofs drowned his voice, and in a moment he was out of sight among the trees.

"There's something in those bushes," said Frank, with difficulty restraining his own horse, which seemed determined to follow Johnny, "and who knows but it might be a grizzly?"

"I am quite sure it is," said Archie. "Don't you remember how badly frightened Pete used to be when there was one of those varmints around?"

As Archie said this, the bushes were violently agitated, and the twigs cracked and snapped as if some heavy body was forcing its way through them. The hounds, waiting to hear no more, turned and fled down the path, leaving the boys to themselves. Frank turned and looked at Arthur. Could it be possible that the pale, terror-stricken youth he saw before him was the one who but a few moments ago had boasted so loudly of his courage? That noise in the bushes had produced a great change in him.

CHAPTER X

ARTHUR SHOWS HIS COURAGE

It must not be supposed that Frank and Archie were entirely unmoved by what had just happened. The strange conduct of the hounds, and the desperate flight of Johnny's horse, were enough to satisfy them that there was some dangerous animal in the bushes in front of them, and the uncertainty of what that animal might be, caused them no little uneasiness. Grizzly bears were frequently met with among the mountains, and they sometimes extended their excursions into the plains, occasioning a general stampede among the stock of the nearest ranch. The grizzly is as much the king of beasts in his own country as the lion in Africa and Asia; and Frank and Archie, during their sojourn at the Old Bear's Hole, had become well enough acquainted with his habits and disposition to know that, if their enemy in the bushes belonged to that species, they were in a dangerous neighborhood. The grizzly might, at any moment, assume the offensive, and in that event, if their horses became entangled in the bushes, or were rendered unmanageable by fright, their destruction was certain. This knowledge caused their hearts to beat a trifle faster than usual, and Frank's hand trembled a little as he unbuckled the holsters in front of his saddle, and grasped one of his revolvers. But neither he nor Archie had any intention of discontinuing their journey, or of leaving the field without having at least one shot at the animal, whatever it might be.

"Now, boys," said Frank, in an excited whisper, "we have a

splendid chance to immortalize ourselves. If that is a grizzly, and we should be fortunate enough to kill him, it would be something worth bragging about, wouldn't it? If I only had my rifle!"

"We must rely upon our friend, here," said Archie. "It's lucky that he is with us, for he is an old hunter, and he won't mind riding into the bushes, and driving him out - will you, Arthur?"

"Eh!" exclaimed that young gentleman, who trembled so violently that he could scarcely hold his reins.

"I say, that, as you are the most experienced in such matters, we shall be obliged to depend upon you to drive the bear out of the bushes into open ground," repeated Archie, who did not appear to notice his friend's trepidation. "We can't all go in there to attack him, for he would be sure to catch some of us. What have you in that gun?"

"B-u-c-k-s-h-o-t," replied Arthur, in an almost inaudible voice. "Let's go home."

"Go home!" exclaimed Frank; "and without even one shot at that fellow! No, sir. You've got the only gun in the party, and, of course, you are the one to attack him. Go right up the path, and when you see him, bang away."

"How big is he?" asked Arthur.

"Why, if he is a full-grown grizzly, he is as big as a cow."

"Will he fight much?"

"I should say he would," answered Archie, who was somewhat surprised at these questions. "Have you forgotten the one you killed with your knife? He will be certain to follow you, if you don't disable him at the first shot, but he can't catch your horse. Besides, as soon as he comes in sight, Frank and I will give him a volley from our revolvers. You are not afraid?"

"Afraid!" repeated Arthur, compressing his lips, and scowling fiercely. "O, no."

"Well, then, make haste," said Frank, who was beginning to get impatient. "Ride up within ten paces of him, and let him have it. That's the way you used to serve the lions in Europe."

"Yes, go on," urged Archie; and he gave Arthur's horse a cut with his whip, to hurry him up.

"O, stop that!" whined Arthur, as the horse sprang forward so suddenly that his rider was nearly unseated. "I am going home."

What might have happened next, it is impossible to tell, had not the boys' attention been turned from Arthur by the yelping of a dog in the bushes a short distance up the mountain.

"That's Carlo," exclaimed Archie. "Now we will soon know what sort of an enemy we have to deal with."

The dog was evidently following the trail of the bear, for he broke out into a continuous baying, which grew louder and fiercer as he approached. The bear heard it, and was either making efforts to escape, or preparing to defend himself; for he thrashed about among the bushes in a way that quite bewildered Frank and Archie, who drew their revolvers, and turned their horses' heads down the path, ready to fight or run, as they might find it necessary. An instant afterward, a large, tan-colored hound bounded across the path, and dashed into the bushes where the game was concealed. It was not one of those which had so disgracefully left the field a few moments before - it was Carlo, Johnny's favorite hound - an animal whose strength had been tested in many a desperate encounter, and which had never been found wanting in courage. Scarcely had he disappeared when Marmion came in sight, also following the trail. He ran with his nose close to the ground, the hair on his back standing straight up like the quills on a porcupine, and his whole appearance indicating great rage and excitement.

"Hi! hi!" yelled Frank. "Take hold of him, you rascal! Now's your time, Arthur. Ride up and give him the contents of your double-barrel; only, be careful, and don't shoot the dogs."

For an instant, it seemed as if Arthur's courage had returned, and that he was about to yield to the entreaties of his companions. He straightened up in his saddle, and, assuming what he, no doubt, imagined to be a very determined look, was on the point of urging his horse forward, when suddenly there arose from the woods a chorus of yells, and snarls, and growls, that made the cold chills creep all over him, and caused him to forget every thing in the desire to put a safe distance between himself and the terrible animal in the bushes. Acting on the impulse of the moment, he wheeled his horse, and, before Frank or Archie could utter a word, he shot by them, and disappeared down the path.

For a moment, the two boys, forgetting that a furious battle was going on a little way from them, gazed at each other in blank amazement. The mighty hunter, who had boasted of whipping a grizzly-bear in a fair fight, with no weapon but his knife, had fled ingloriously, without having seen any thing to be frightened at.

"That's one lie nailed," said Frank.

"More than one, I should think," returned Archie, contemptuously. "I shall have nothing more to do with that fellow. This is the end of my acquaintance with him."

No doubt Archie was in earnest when he said this; but, had he been able to look into the future, he would have discovered that he was destined to have a great deal more to do with Arthur Vane. Instead of being the end of his acquaintance with that young gentleman, it was only the beginning of it.

Meanwhile, the fight in the bushes, desperate as it was, judging by the noise it occasioned, was ended, and Arthur had scarcely disappeared when Marmion and Carlo walked out into the path, and, after looking up at the boys, and giving their tails a few jerks, as if to say "We've done it!" seated themselves on their haunches, and awaited further orders. Archie threw his reins to his cousin, and, springing out of his saddle, went forward to survey the scene of the conflict. He was gone but a moment, and when he came out of the bushes, he was dragging after him - not a grizzly bear, but a large gray wolf, which had been overpowered and killed by the dogs. One of the wolf's hind-legs was caught in a trap, to which was fastened a short piece of chain and a clog. The animal had doubtless been paying his respects to some sheep-fold during the night, and had put his foot into the trap while searching for his supper. He had retreated toward the mountains, and had dragged the trap until the clog caught, and held him fast. That was the reason he did not run off when the boys came up, and the commotion in the bushes had been caused by his efforts to free himself.

While the boys were examining their prize, Johnny, having succeeded in stopping his frantic horse, was returning to the place from which he had started on his involuntary ride. As he was about to enter the woods at the base of the mountains, he saw a horse emerge from the trees, and come toward him at a rapid gallop. His bridle was flying loose in the wind, and Johnny at first thought he was running away; but a second glance showed him that there was somebody on his back.

"Stampeded," thought Johnny. "If I am laughed at, it will be some consolation to know that I am not alone in my misery."

The rider of the stampeded horse was bent almost double; his feet were out of the stirrups, which were being thrown wildly about; both hands were holding fast to the horn of the saddle; his face was deadly pale, and, altogether, he presented the appearance of one who had been thoroughly alarmed. Although he looked very unlike the dignified Arthur Vane, who had ridden so gayly over that road but a few moments before, Johnny recognized him at once; and the first thought that flashed through his mind was that something terrible had happened to Frank and Archie.

"What's the matter?" asked Johnny, pulling up his horse with a jerk.

"Grizzly bears!" shouted Arthur, in reply, without attempting to check his headlong flight.

"Grizzly bears!" echoed Johnny, in dismay. "And are you going off without trying to help those boys? Stop, and go back with me."

But Arthur was past stopping, either by ability or inclination. Digging his spurs into the sides of his horse, which was already going at the top of his speed, he went by Johnny like the wind, and in a moment was so far away that it was useless to make any further attempts to stop him. For an instant, Johnny was irresolute; then he turned in his saddle, and shouted one word, which the wind caught up and carried to the ears of the flying horseman, and which did much to bring about the events we have yet to describe.

"*Coward!*" yelled Johnny, with all the strength of his lungs.

Having thus given utterance to his opinion of Arthur Vane, he put spurs to his horse and galloped into the woods, hoping to reach the scene of the conflict in time to be of service to his friends. But, as we know, the grizzly bear had proved to be a wolf, and had already been killed by the dogs.

CHAPTER XI

ARTHUR PLANS REVENGE

Meanwhile, Arthur Vane continued his mad flight toward the settlement. His hat was gone, his fine shot-gun had been thrown aside as a useless incumbrance, and his tomahawk and knife had dropped out of his belt; but he was too frightened to stop to pick them up. No pause he knew until he reached Mr. Harris's rancho, where he reined up his panting horse, and electrified the family by shouting through the open window:

"Grizzly bears! Grizzly bears!"

"Where?" breathlessly inquired Mr. Harris, running out on the porch.

Before Arthur could reply, Johnny's mother appeared; and a single glance at the frightened hunter and his dripping steed, was enough to awaken in her mind the most terrible apprehensions. She knew, instinctively, that something dreadful had happened.

"O, my son!" she screamed, sinking down on the porch, and covering her face with her hands.

Mr. Harris did not stop to ask any questions then. He knew the route the boys had taken in the morning, and his first thought was to start for the scene of the conflict, although he had little hopes of arriving in time to be of any assistance to

Harry Castlemon

the young hunters.

"Jose!" he shouted to one of his Rancheros, who happened to pass by the house at that moment, "call all the men to saddle up at once. The boys have been attacked by a grizzly in the mountains."

The gentleman carried his fainting wife into the house, and presently re-appeared with a brace of revolvers strapped to his waist, and a rifle in his hand.

"Did you see any of the boys hurt?"

He asked this question in a firm voice; but his pale face and quivering lips showed that the news he had just received had not been without its effect upon him.

"No, sir," replied Arthur. "My horse ran away with me; but I heard the fight, and I know that the dogs were all cut to pieces. The bear was an awful monster - as large as an ox; and such teeth and claws as he had! I never saw the like in all my hunting."

In a few moments, half a dozen herdsmen, all well armed, galloped up, one of them leading his employer's horse.

"Vane," said Mr. Harris, as he sprang into his saddle, "you will stop on your way home, and tell Mr. Winters, will you not?"

Arthur replied by putting spurs to his horse, and in a few moments he was standing in Mr. Winters's court, spreading consternation among the people of the rancho. Dick and Bob were there; but, unlike the rest of the herdsmen, they seemed to be but little affected by Arthur's story.

"You'll never see those boys again," said the latter, winding up his narrative with a description of the bear by which they had been attacked.

"Now, don't you be anyways oneasy," replied Dick, hurrying off to saddle his horse. "If it war a grizzly, he's dead enough by this time, for I knowed them youngsters long afore you sot eyes on to 'em, an' I know what they can do. Didn't I tell you, 'Squire," he added, turning to Mr. Winters, who was pacing anxiously up and down the porch, "that Frank would come out all right when he war stampeded with them buffaler? Wal, I tell you the same now."

Arthur remained at the rancho until Uncle James and his herdsmen set out for the mountains, and then turned his face homeward.

It is a rule that seldom fails, that when one meets a bragga-docio, he can put him down as a coward. We have seen that it held good in Arthur's case; for, although he had not caught the smallest glimpse of the animal in the bushes, he was so terrified that he had run his horse eight miles; and, while he was plunging his spurs into the gray's sides at almost every jump, he imagined that the animal was running away with him. He was so badly frightened that he did not pause to consider that he might have occasioned a great deal of unnecessary anxiety and alarm by the stories he had circulated. He really believed that every word he had uttered was the truth; and he reached this conclusion by a process of reasoning perfectly satisfactory to himself. He had heard the growls and snarls uttered by the animal in the bushes, when attacked by the dogs, and they were so appalling, that he felt safe in believing that they came from some terrible monster. The conduct of the hounds, and of Johnny's horse, confirmed this opinion. Besides, Frank and Archie had pronounced the animal a grizzly, and Arthur was quite sure it was; for nothing else, except a lion or tiger, could have uttered such growls. He had heard that grizzlies were very tenacious of life, and hard to whip, and, consequently, it followed, as a thing of course, that Frank and Archie, and the dogs, were utterly annihilated.

"I'm safe, thank goodness!" said Arthur, to himself. "If those fellows were foolish enough to stay there and be clawed to pieces, that's their lookout and not mine. Johnny Harris insulted me by calling me a coward. He may escape from the bear, and if he does, I shall think up a plan to punish him."

When Arthur reached home, he repeated his story as he had told it to Mr. Harris and Uncle James, and he straightway found himself a hero. He had seen a grizzly bear with terrible claws, and a frightful array of teeth; his horse had run away with him, and carried him eight miles before he could stop him, and he had come home with a whole skin. It was wonderful.

Arthur threw on airs accordingly. He strutted about among the herdsmen, and entertained his servant, a Mexican boy about his own age, named Pedro, with a description of the fight, in which he had seen four fierce dogs completely demolished.

Pedro complimented him highly, and the Rancheros called him a brave lad - although Arthur himself failed to see what he had done that was deserving of praise. He went to bed in excellent spirits, and was awakened in the morning, about daylight, by Pedro, who came into his room, carrying in his hand a double-barreled shot-gun, a tomahawk, and sheath-knife, and, under his arm, he held a hat, and a bundle wrapped up in a newspaper. Pedro held his sombrero over his face, so that nothing could be seen but his eyes, which were brimful of laughter.

"Now, then," exclaimed Arthur, raising himself on his elbow, and looking fiercely at the boy, "what do you want in here at this barbarous hour, and what are you grinning at?"

"Why, sir - the bear, you know; it wasn't a bear after all," stammered Pedro, in reply.

"It wasn't! I say it was. Didn't I see him with my own eyes, and hear him growl with my own ears? Take that hat down from your face, and stop your laughing."

Pedro obeyed. He placed the bundle on a chair beside the bed, leaned the gun up in one corner, deposited the other articles upon the table, and then pulled out of his pocket a note which he handed to Arthur.

"Now take yourself off," commanded that young gentleman.

Pedro vanished, and Arthur heard him laughing to himself as he passed through the hall.

"What does the rascal mean, I wonder; and who can be writing to me so early in the morning?"

Arthur looked at the bundle, which lay on the chair beside him, felt of it with his fingers, and then turned his attention to the note, which ran as follows:

> "Frank, Archie, and Johnny present their compliments to Colonel Vane, and beg leave to inform him that, after a struggle unequaled in the annals of hunting, they succeeded in dispatching the monster by which they were attacked yesterday. They are, also, happy to announce that the dogs, which were so badly cut up during the fight, have so far recovered as to be out, and to take their regular rations. They request the Colonel to accept the accompanying articles, including the skin of the grizzly bear, and to preserve them as mementoes of the most exciting event of his life. They sincerely hope that the Colonel sustained no injury during his ride on his runaway horse."

Arthur read this letter over twice, and, although he made no comments upon it, it was easy enough to see that he was highly enraged. He sat up in the bed, and, with trembling hands, tore off the covering of the bundle, and discovered the skin of the gray wolf.

"By gracious!" exclaimed Arthur, jumping out on the floor. "Was a gentleman ever before so insulted? That little Yankee,

Archie Winters, is at the bottom of all this, and if he don't suffer for it, I'll know the reason why."

He tore the note into fragments, pitched the bundle out of the window, and walked angrily about the room, shaking his fists in the air, and threatening all sorts of vengeance against Archie and his two friends. If he had been in his sober senses, he would have felt heartily ashamed of himself; but the note had opened his eyes to the fact that he had sadly injured his reputation, and he was angry at his companions because he had done so - although how they could be blamed for that, it would have puzzled a sensible boy to determine. But, after all, his case was not an isolated one. It is by no means uncommon for boys, when they get angry, to revenge themselves upon some innocent thing. We remember that, on a certain rainy day, several boys were congregated in a barn, amusing themselves by turning hand-springs. One clumsy fellow, whose feet were so heavy that he could not get them over his head, became greatly enraged at his failures, and finally tried to soothe his wounded pride by whipping one of his companions.

Arthur was actuated by the same spirit. He walked up and down his room for a long time, trying to make up his mind what he should do, and, when he was called to breakfast, he had decided upon a plan of operations, which promised to make Archie and his friends a great deal of trouble.

"I'll be revenged upon the whole lot of them at once," said Arthur, to himself. "Upon Johnny Harris, for calling me a coward; upon Archie Winters, for writing me that note - for I know he did it, although Johnny's name does come last - and upon Frank Nelson, for being a friend to those fellows, and for being so stuck up. He scarcely spoke to me yesterday, and I won't stand such treatment from any boy. I'll teach these backwoodsmen to insult a gentleman!"

"Well, Arthur," said Mr. Vane, as the boy seated himself at the table, "you must have looked through a very badly-frightened pair of eyes, to make a grizzly bear out of a wolf."

"Who told you it was a wolf?" asked Arthur, gruffly.

"One of Mr. Winters's herdsmen - Dick Lewis, I believe, they call him. He came over this morning to bring your weapons and hat."

Dick despised a coward quite as much as he admired a boy of spirit and courage, and it is certain that the story, as he had heard it from Frank and Archie, lost nothing in passing through his hands. He first told it to Mr. Vane, as he handed him the articles he had brought, and then repeated it to one of the Rancheros; and, by the time Arthur had finished his breakfast, the occurrences of the previous day were known to every one on the rancho. Pedro laughed when he brought out Arthur's horse, and the herdsmen, as he rode through their quarters, exchanged winks with one another, and made a great many remarks about grizzly bears, especially concerning the one Arthur had seen the day before. There was one man, however, who took no part in the joking and laughing, and that was Joaquin, who was just mounting his horse to drive up some stock.

"Don't mind them," said he, as Arthur rode beside him. "They are a set of blackguards, and don't know how to treat a gentleman."

"Now, that's like a true friend," replied Arthur. "You're the only one I have on the ranch."

Joaquin was a villainous-looking Mexican, and since he had been in Mr. Vane's employ, he had had little to do with the other herdsmen. He seemed to prefer to be alone, unless he could have Arthur for company. He always took a great deal of interest in the boy's affairs, and it was from his lips that Arthur had heard the story of Frank's adventures with Pierre Costello. Joaquin had gained Arthur's good will by confiding to him a great many secrets, and one day he went so far as to confess that Pierre was his particular friend, and that, if he felt so disposed, he could point out the cave in the mountains where the robber was concealed, and tell who it was that supplied him with food, and kept him posted in all that happened in the settlement. Joaquin might have added, further, that he himself had held several long interviews with Pierre of late, and had talked over with him certain plans, in which Arthur Vane and his three companions of the previous day bore prominent parts. But this was one secret that the Ranchero kept to himself.

"If you know where the robber is hidden, why don't you tell Mr. Winters, and claim the reward?" Arthur had one day asked Joaquin.

"What! betray my best friend!" exclaimed that worthy, in great astonishment. "I am not base enough to abuse any man's confidence. Do you suppose that if you were in Pierre's place, and I knew where you were concealed, that I could be hired to play false to you? No, sir!"

Arthur remembered this remark, and on this particular morning, as he rode out with the Ranchero, he called the latter's attention to it, and asked if he could trust him. The reply was a strong affirmative, which satisfied Arthur that he might speak freely, and the result was, the revelation of his plan for taking revenge on Frank, Johnny, and Archie. Joaquin listened attentively, and Arthur was delighted at the readiness, and even eagerness, with which the herdsman fell in with his ideas, and promised his assistance. He had one amendment to propose, that did not exactly suit Arthur; but, after a little argument, he agreed to it. They talked the matter over for half an hour, and then Arthur started for home, and the Ranchero galloped off to attend to his stock.

That night, after all his companions were asleep, Joaquin crept quietly out of his quarters, and, after saddling his horse, rode toward the mountains. He was gone nearly all night, but returned in time to get to bed before the herdsmen awoke; and, when he arose with the others, none of them knew that he had been away from the rancho. Arthur Vane must have known something about it, however, for the next morning, as soon as he had eaten his breakfast, he mounted his horse, and overtook Joaquin, just as he was leaving his quarters.

"Well!" said Arthur.

The Ranchero looked suspiciously about him, and, finding that there was no one within sight or hearing, he detached his knife and sheath from his belt, produced a folded paper from the crown of his sombrero, and handed them both to Arthur, saying, in a suppressed whisper:

"It's all right."

"Did you see him?" asked Arthur, eagerly.

"I did, and he says your plan is an excellent one, and he will help you to carry it out. The black line on that paper points out the road you are to follow; the light lines, that branch off from it, are old bridle-paths. Look at the paper often, and you can't get lost. He has never seen you, you know, and, when you find him, you must show him my knife to prove that you are a friend. Bear one thing in mind, now, and that is, you are playing a dangerous game, and if you are found out, the country around here will be too hot to hold you. Remember that I am your only friend in this matter, and say nothing to nobody except me."

With this piece of advice, the Ranchero galloped off, and Arthur, after placing the knife in his belt, and putting the paper carefully away in his pocket, rode toward the mountains.

During the next few hours, Arthur consulted his paper frequently, and, about noon, he was standing at the base of a precipitous cliff, twenty miles from home, examining the natural features of the place, and comparing them with his diagram. He saw no one; but half way up the cliff was a huge bowlder, over which peered a pair of eyes that were closely watching every move he made; and, when Arthur whistled

Harry Castlemon

twice, the eyes disappeared, and a man stepped from behind the rock, and said, in a gruff voice:

"Who are you, and what do you want here?"

"Are you Pierre Costello?" asked Arthur.

"Well, now, that's no concern of yours," replied the man. "Who are you?" As he spoke, he drew a revolver from his sash, and rested it on the rock beside him, the muzzle pointing straight at the boy's head.

"Don't!" cried Arthur, turning pale, and stepping back. "I am Arthur Vane, and I have come here to have a talk with you. Here is Joaquin's knife, which will prove that I am all right."

The man returned his revolver to his belt, and came down the cliff; and, presently, Arthur found himself standing face to face with a live robber.

"I am Pierre Costello," said the latter; "and I was waiting for you."

CHAPTER XII

OFF FOR THE MOUNTAINS

Arthur looked at the robber with curiosity. Yellow-covered novels had always been his favorite reading, and highwaymen, brigands, and pirates were, in his estimation, the only heroes worthy of emulation. Pierre, but for one thing, would have come up to his beau ideal of a robber. He was loaded with weapons, and he was tall and broad-shouldered, sported a ferocious mustache, and his hair fell down upon his shoulders. He was dressed in the gayest Mexican style, but his clothing had seen long service, and was not quite as neat as Arthur would have liked to have seen it. It was plain that Pierre did not waste much time upon his toilet; but, after all, he was a very good-looking villain.

The robber was quite as much interested in his visitor as the latter was in him. He had often heard of Arthur through Joaquin; and, if the boy had known all Pierre's intentions concerning him, he might not have felt quite so much at his ease.

"I can't spare much time," said the robber, breaking the silence at last.

"Nor I either," returned Arthur; "so I will begin my business at once, and get through as soon as I can. I have heard the particulars of your fights with Frank Nelson, and I propose to put you in the way of making five times the amount of money you would have made if you had captured him when you met him in the mountains. I want to be revenged upon Frank and his crowd, for they have grossly insulted me."

"Of course they have," said Pierre. "I know all about it."

"I can't punish them by myself," continued Arthur, "for they are three to my one. I am not afraid of Johnny Harris, or Archie Winters; but there's that other Yankee, Frank Nelson. He is as strong as a lion, and if he once gets his blood up, he don't care for any thing. I am afraid of him."

"I don't wonder at it. I have had some experience with him, and, if he had a few more years on his shoulders, I should be afraid of him myself."

"I can't punish them unless I have help," repeated Arthur; "and, if you will lend me your assistance, you can make sixty thousand dollars by it. I heard those fellows say, yesterday, that they are going on a hunting expedition, next week. I will make friends with them again, and find out when they intend to start, and I propose that you capture them, and take them to some safe place in the mountains, and demand twenty thousand dollars apiece for them. You can demand more, if you choose, and get it, too; for Mr. Harris is rich, and so is Mr. Winters. You must have some men to assist you, however."

"I understand that," said Pierre. "I'll find the men."

"Will you do it?"

"Certainly, I will."

"Give me your hand, Pierre; I knew you would help me. But let me tell you one thing, and that is, when you capture them you must look out for yourself. They will have plenty of weapons, and, from what I have seen of them, I don't think they would hesitate to use them if they got a chance. There's one thing about this business I don't exactly admire. Of course, I shall start with their expedition - I want to have the satisfaction of seeing them captured - and my idea was, that, when you made the attack on them, you should give me a chance to escape; but Joaquin says, that won't do at all."

"Certainly not;" said Pierre, quickly. "I shall have five men with me, and if we should let you get away, the boys would be suspicious of you at once."

"That's just what Joaquin said; and since I have thought the matter over, I have come to the conclusion that he was right. I don't want them to know that I had a hand in this matter, for they might make me some trouble."

"Very likely they would. You must allow yourself to be captured with the others."

"Well, I sha'n't mind that, for, I believe, I can enjoy myself among the mountains for a month or two. But, Pierre, when you get them you must hold fast to them."

"I am not the man to let sixty thousand dollars slip through my fingers," said the Ranchero, with a laugh.

"And there are three other things I want you to remember," continued Arthur, earnestly. "The first is, you must not demand any ransom for me."

"Oh no; of course not."

"The second is, I shall expect to be treated at all times like a visitor. I am a gentleman, and a gentleman's son."

"I am well aware of that fact. I knew it the moment I put my eyes on you."

"The third thing I want you to bear in mind, is, that I shall not be captured without a struggle; and that every chance I get I shall try to escape. I am going to show those fellows that I have some spunk. I want you to act natural, and to prevent me from getting away from you; but you must not abuse me. You can treat the others as roughly as you please. Do you agree to all this?"

"I do, and there's my hand on it," said Pierre. "I fully understand your plans now, and know just what you want me to do; and, what's more, I'll do it. If you have got through with what you have to say, you had better be off. I have a good many enemies, and I am in danger as long as you are here. Watch those boys closely, and keep Joaquin posted. I can find out every thing I want to know from him."

"My plans are working nicely," chuckled Arthur, as he rode homeward. "I'll teach these backwoodsmen manners, before I am done with them."

"Eighty thousand dollars!" said Pierre, gazing after the retreating horseman. "That's a nice little sum to be divided among six of us."

This remark will show whether or not the robber intended to abide by the promises he had just made to Arthur Vane; and, while we are on this subject, it may not be amiss to say, that the scheme Arthur had proposed, was one on which the robber had been meditating for many days. During the time he had lived in the mountains, he had kept his brain busy, and had been allowed ample opportunity to decide upon his future operations. He had been astonished and enraged at his failure to secure the twelve thousand dollars, and to make Frank Nelson a prisoner, and he had resolved to make amends for his defeat by capturing Frank and all his companions, including Arthur Vane. Pierre had plenty of friends to assist him, but there was one question that troubled him, and presented an obstacle that he could see no way to overcome; and that was, how to capture all the boys at once. That must be done, or his plan would fail. He could get his hands upon Arthur Vane at any time; but the others were like birds on the wing - here to-day, and miles away to-morrow - and Pierre did not know where to find them. Now, however, the difficulty was removed. Frank and his friends were going on a hunting expedition, Arthur would ascertain when they were going to start, and what road they intended to take, and when the day arrived, the robber could call in his men, who were employed on the neighboring ranchos, and capture the boys without the least trouble. Pierre was very glad that Arthur had got angry at Frank.

Meanwhile Frank, Archie, and Johnny, all unconscious of the plans that were being formed against them, enjoyed themselves to the utmost, and wasted a good deal of time every day in laughing over the incidents that had transpired during their ride to Captain Porter's ranch. Archie, especially, had a great deal to say about it. He had an accomplishment, of which we have never before had occasion to speak: he was a first-class mimic; and he took no little pride in showing off his powers. He could imitate the brogue of an Irishman the broken English of a Dutchman, or the nasal twang of a Yankee, to perfection; and one day, while he was in the barn saddling his horse, he carried on a lengthy conversation with Bob Kelly (who was on the outside of the building), about some runaway cattle, and the old trapper thought all the while that he was talking to his chum, Dick Lewis. Now Archie had a new subject to practice upon. He laid himself out to personate Arthur Vane; and he not only successfully imitated that young gentleman's pompous style of talking, and his dignified manner of riding and walking, but even the tone of his voice. He criticised Frank and Johnny continually, and made them laugh, till their jaws ached, by recounting imaginary adventures on the burning sands of Patagonia, and among the icebergs and polar bears of India.

The day following the one on which Arthur Vane visited the robber in the mountains, found the three boys on the back porch of Mr. Winters's rancho, making preparations for their hunting expedition. Frank was cleaning his rifle, and Archie and Johnny were repairing an old pack-saddle, in which they intended to carry their provisions and extra ammunition. Archie was seated on the floor, with an awl in one hand, and a piece of stout twine in the other; and, while he was working at the pack-saddle, his tongue was moving rapidly.

"I am young in years, fellows," he was saying, "but I am aged in experience. If I had my rights, I should long ago have been gray-headed. I have seen thrilling times in my life, and have been the hero of adventures, that, were I to relate them to you, would make each particular hair of your heads stand on end, like the quills of a punched hedge-hog. I am - if you will kindly permit me to use a slang expression - an old hand at the business of hunting and trapping, and have accomplishments in which I can not be beaten. Among them, stands my ability to whip a grizzly bear in a fair fight, with no weapon but my knife. I have hunted wild gorillas in the streets of New York City; have" -

"Good morning, fellows!"

Archie brought the story of his adventures to a sudden close, and, looking over his shoulder, saw Arthur Vane standing at the end of the porch. The boys had never expected him to call upon them again, and Archie and Johnny were too surprised to speak; but Frank, who always kept his wits about him, returned Arthur's greeting, and invited him to occupy the chair he pushed toward him. He was not at all pleased to see the visitor, but he was too much of a gentleman to show it.

One would suppose, that the remembrance of what had happened, three days before, would have caused Arthur some embarrassment; but such was not the case. On the contrary, he was as dignified as ever, and seemed to be perfectly at his ease. Frank and his friends were considerate enough to refrain from making any allusions to the fright he had sustained, but Arthur brought the subject up himself.

"I received your note," said he, "and also the articles you were kind enough to send me; and I am here now to say, that I feel heartily ashamed of myself. From some cause or another, that I could not explain if I should try, I was extremely nervous that day; but I may, some time, have an opportunity to show you that I am not as much of a coward as I know you now believe me to be."

Arthur remained at the rancho all that day, sitting down at the same, table, and eating his dinner with the boys he was about to betray into the hands of the robbers; and, when he went home that night, he had asked, and received, permission to accompany them to the mountains. Their consent had been given reluctantly, and with very bad grace; but they could see no way to get around it. Arthur was a boy with whom they did not care to associate; but he had done them no injury, and they could not bring themselves to refuse his request.

"They will start early Monday morning," soliloquized Arthur, as he rode homeward, "and will take the road that leads to Captain Porter's. This is Friday. I shall send word by Joaquin to Pierre to-night, and he will have plenty of time to make all his arrangements."

Arthur spent the next day with the boys at Mr. Winters's rancho, and, when he rode over on Monday morning, he brought with him a supply of provisions, which were stowed away in the pack-saddle with the rest. Frank and his friends had been waiting for him, and now that they were all ready, they mounted their horses and rode off - Archie leading an extra horse, which carried the pack-saddle. As they galloped through the Rancheros' quarters, Dick appeared at the door of his cabin, and shouted after them words, which, taken in connection with the events that were about to transpire, seemed like prophecy.

"You'll be wishin' fur me an' Bob, to get you out of the hands of that ar' greaser, afore you're two days older," yelled Dick.

"You don't suppose that we four fellows will let one man capture us, do you?" shouted Archie, in reply. "If we do get into trouble, and you find it out, you'll come to our rescue, won't you?"

"Sartin. Now, don't be keerless, like you allers are."

The boys kept their horses in a rapid gallop until they reached the bridle-path in the mountains, and then Archie went ahead with the pack-horse, and the others followed in single file. They rode along singing and shouting, and little dreaming of the danger that was so near, until they arrived in sight of the spring, near which Frank had his last encounter with the robber. He soon found that he was to have another adventure there; for, as he and his companions rode toward the spring, they were startled by a shrill whistle, which echoed among the mountains, and was answered on all sides of them; and, before they had recovered from their surprise, Pierre Costello appeared in the path, as suddenly as though he had dropped from the clouds, and came toward them, holding a pistol in each hand.

"Halt!" shouted the robber.

The boys looked about them, as if seeking some avenue of escape, and then they saw that Pierre was not alone. Every thicket, toward which they turned their eyes, bristled with weapons, and a dozen revolvers were leveled straight at their heads. It was useless to think of flight.

CHAPTER XIII

PIERRE AND HIS BAND

"Halt, I say!" repeated Pierre, riding up beside Frank, and seizing his horse by the bridle. "Disarm them, men, and shoot down the first one that resists," he added, as the band closed up around the boys.

Frank, seeing, at a glance, that it was useless to think of escape, sat quietly in his saddle, and allowed Pierre to take possession of his rifle, pistols, and lasso.

Johnny and Archie also surrendered at discretion; but Arthur, believing that the time had come to retrieve the reputation he had lost so ingloriously a few days before, determined that he would not surrender without a fight. It was a part of his contract with the robber chief, that he should be allowed to resist as desperately as he pleased, and he took advantage of it. He gazed at the Rancheros for a moment with well-assumed astonishment, and then, appearing to comprehend the situation, he shouted:

"Stick together, fellows, and fight for your liberties! Don't give up, like a pack of cowards! Knock 'em down! Shoot 'em! Take your hand off that bridle, you villain!"

As Arthur spoke, he dashed his spurs into the flanks of his horse, which bounded forward so suddenly, that he jerked the bridle from the grasp of the Ranchero who was holding him.

Harry Castlemon

"Hurrah! I'm free, boys!" he shouted, clubbing his gun, and swinging it around his head. "Follow me, and I'll show you how we used to clean out the Indians."

Arthur's triumph was of short duration. The Ranchero, from whom he had escaped, was at his side in an instant, and, again seizing his bridle with one hand, he leveled a pistol full at his prisoner's head with the other, while Pierre caught his gun from behind, and wrested it from his grasp. At the same moment, a lasso, thrown by the Ranchero who had taken charge of Archie, settled down over his shoulders, and was drawn tight.

Pierre and his band were obeying their instructions to the very letter, indeed, they were altogether too zealous in their efforts to appear "natural," and Arthur began to be suspicious that they were in sober earnest with him, as well as with the others. He looked up into Pierre's face, in the hope of receiving from him some friendly token - a sly wink or a nod, which would satisfy him that he was "all right," and in no danger of receiving bodily injury; but he saw nothing of the kind. The chieftain's face wore a terrible scowl, and he even lifted Arthur's gun above his head, as if he had half a mind to knock him out of his saddle.

"Quarter! quarter!" gasped Arthur, striving, with nervous fingers, to pull the lasso from his neck, and beginning to be thoroughly alarmed. "I surrender."

"Well, let that be your last attempt at escape," said Pierre, in a very savage tone of voice, "or you will find, to your cost, that we are not to be trifled with."

In the meantime, the other Rancheros, while holding fast to their prisoners, had relieved them of their weapons; and, as soon as Pierre had seen Arthur conquered, he seized the bridle of the pack-horse, while each of the other members of the band took charge of one of the boys, and the cavalcade started down the ravine at a rapid gallop.

All this happened in much less time than we have taken to describe it. Before the young hunters had fairly recovered from the astonishment caused by the sudden appearance of Pierre and his band, they had been disarmed, and were being led captive into the mountains.

Frank and his two friends were more bewildered than alarmed. The whole thing was so unexpected, and had been accomplished so quickly and quietly! Remembering the particulars of Frank's previous encounter with Pierre Costello, they did not stand in fear of bodily harm. Although they had not the slightest suspicion that their capture was the result of treachery on the part of Arthur Vane, they well understood the motives of the robbers, and knew, as well as if Pierre had explained the matter to them, that they were to be used as a means to extort money from their relatives, and that they had nothing to fear, so long as they submitted quietly to their enemies. But this was something that one of the three boys, at least, had no intention of doing. Frank's brain was already busy with plans for escape. He had twice beaten Pierre at his own game, and, if the robber did not keep his wits about him, he would do it again. As for Arthur, although his plans were, thus far, as successful as he could have desired, he was very much disappointed. The three boys, who had dared to hold him up to the people of the settlement in his true character, were prisoners, and he had Pierre's assurance that they would remain such until the demands he intended to make upon their relatives should be complied with. But, after all, Arthur did not experience the satisfaction he had hoped he would, for the robbers had treated him very roughly. The chief had raised his own gun over his head; another had choked him with his lasso, and a third had pointed a loaded pistol at him. That was a nice way to treat a visitor! Arthur began to wish that he had never had any thing to do with Pierre and his band.

The chief, who rode in advance with the pack-horse, led the way at a break-neck pace, and the boys, being one behind the other, each in company with the Ranchero who had him in charge, were allowed no opportunity to converse with one another, even had they desired it. Frank, for want of something better to do, began to make an examination of the members of the band. Like their leader, they were full-blooded Mexicans, with enormous mustaches, and long, tangled hair, which looked as though it had never seen a comb. They were dressed in gay-colored clothes - blue jackets, buckskin pants, very wide at the knee, and covered with buttons, ribbons, and gold lace. They wore long sashes around their waists, which were thrust full of bowie-knives and revolvers. They carried short, heavy rifles, slung over their shoulders by leather bands, and behind their saddles were their ponchos, which did duty both as overcoats and beds. Taken altogether, they were a hard-looking set, and seemed capable of any atrocity. The man who had charge of Frank was particularly noticeable in this respect, and our hero thought that all he needed were the leggins, and high-pointed hat, to make him a first-class brigand. This man kept a sharp eye upon his prisoner, and scowled at him, as if he regarded him as his most implacable foe.

"You needn't look so mad," said Frank, at length. "I don't remember that I ever did you any harm, and I certainly am not foolish enough to try to escape, as long as you keep hold of my bridle."

"You had better not," said the Ranchero, smiling grimly, and shaking his head in a very threatening manner.

"I don't know that you can frighten me," returned Frank, coolly. "I wish I was a man for about five minutes."

"What would you do?" asked the Ranchero, who seemed to be pleased, as well as astonished, at the boy's courage and independence.

"I'd make your head and your heels change places in a great hurry. In other words, I'd knock you out of your saddle. Then I'd say: 'Good-by, Mr. - Mr.' - what's your name?"

"Mercedes - Antoine Mercedes."

"Well, Mr. Mercedes, I'll never forget that benevolent-looking face of yours. As I was saying, I would bid you good-by, and leave. I'd pass those fellows," he added, jerking his thumb over his shoulder toward the robbers in the rear, "before they could say 'General Jackson' with their mouth's open. You haven't got a horse, in this party, that can catch Roderick."

The Ranchero smiled again, and tapped the butt of one of his revolvers with his finger.

"Oh, you wouldn't have a chance to fire a pistol at me," said Frank, quickly. "By the time you could get on your feet again, after I had knocked you down, I would be a mile from here. Did Pierre ever tell you how nicely I fooled him?" he continued, noticing that the chief was turned half around in his saddle, listening to what he had to say. "Well I am not surprised that he never mentioned it, for he ought to feel ashamed of himself."

"Ay; but I have got you fast this time," said Pierre, with a laugh. "Let us see how nicely you will fool me now. One at a time here, men," he added, in a louder tone, "and keep close watch of those prisoners."

As Pierre spoke, the cavalcade emerged from the woods, and Frank found himself on the brink of a rocky chasm, which stretched away to the right as far as his eye could reach, and seemed to extend down into the very bowels of the earth. It was so deep that his head grew dizzy, as he looked into it. On his left, and directly in front of him, was a precipitous mountain, the top of which hung threateningly over the gorge below. It seemed to Frank that they could go no farther in this direction, until Pierre urged his horse upon a narrow ledge that ran around the base of the cliff. Antoine followed after the pack-horse, and Frank came next. Roderick pricked up his ears, looked over into the gorge, and snorted loudly. He moved very slowly and carefully, and well he might: for a single misstep on his part would have sent both him and his rider to destruction. The path was so narrow that, although Roderick walked on the extreme outer edge, Frank's feet now and then brushed against the rock on the opposite side. Our hero felt his sombrero rise on his head, whenever he looked into the chasm, or allowed himself to reflect how slight an accident might launch him into eternity. But there was no backing out. Once on that ledge, a person must go forward; for there was no room to turn around.

After Frank came another of the band, and Johnny followed at his heels. Archie and his keeper came next, and Arthur and *his* keeper brought up the rear. They all rode fearlessly upon the ledge, until it came Arthur's turn, and then was heard a cry of remonstrance. The young gentleman, who had been brave enough to fill the perilous office of scout among the Indians of the plains, did not possess the courage necessary to carry him through this ordeal. He turned as pale as death, and stopped his horse.

"Go on," sternly commanded his keeper.

"Oh, it's dangerous," returned Arthur, in pitiful tones. "What if my horse should slip off? That gully must be a thousand feet deep!"

"More than that," said Archie, who, although very far from being pleased at his own situation, could not resist the inclination to torment Arthur. "It reaches clear through to India, where you used to hunt polar bears."

"That's so," said Johnny; "for just now, as I looked over into the gorge, I saw a lot of half naked Hindoos tumbling about among the icebergs."

"And I heard them yelling," chimed in Frank; "and saw one of those big white bears after them."

"Go on!" repeated the Ranchero, impatiently.

"O, now, see here!" exclaimed Arthur, in a trembling voice, trying to turn his horse's head away from the pass, "I believe, I'll" -

He was about to say, that he believed he would not go any further, but that he would return home and leave Pierre and his band to take care of his three enemies; but his keeper did not give him time to finish the sentence. Seeing that Arthur had no intention of following the rest of the party, the robber took his lasso from the pommel of his saddle, and with it struck his prisoner's horse a blow that caused the fiery animal to give one tremendous spring, which brought him to the very brink of the precipice. In his efforts to stop himself, a portion of the earth was detached by his hoofs and fell with a loud noise into the abyss, bounding down its rocky sides, and crashing through bushes and branches of trees in its rapid descent to the bottom. The horse, frightened by the sound, and smarting under the blow of the lasso, reared so straight upon his hind legs that he seemed in imminent danger of toppling over into the chasm; and then, for the first time in his life, Arthur found himself in real peril. He screamed loudly, clung to the horn of his saddle with a death grip, and closed his eyes, expecting every instant to find himself whirling through the air toward the bottom of the gorge. But help was near: the strong hand of his keeper grasped the bridle, and brought the horse back upon firm ground.

"Now, then, go on!" commanded the Ranchero, without giving his prisoner time to recover from his fright.

Arthur was powerless to obey, for so great was his terror that he could not move a muscle; but his horse, being left to himself, stepped boldly upon the ledge, and followed after the rest of the party, who had, by this time, disappeared around the base of the mountain.

Harry Castlemon

CHAPTER XIV

A DINNER IN THE MOUNTAINS

Pass Christian - for that was the name of the gorge - was two miles long. About half that distance from the entrance, was a natural recess in the mountains, comprising perhaps half an acre, which was covered with grass and stunted oaks, and watered by a spring that gushed out from under a huge bowlder, which had fallen into the glade from the mountains above. Here the robber chief had decided to remain long enough to send a message to Mr. Winters. The horses had been unsaddled, and were cropping the grass, and the Rancheros were stretched out under the shade of the trees - all except two of their number, one of whom, having lighted a fire, was engaged in cooking the dinner, and the other was standing near the entrance to the glade, leaning on his rifle, and keeping a close watch over the prisoners. Frank and his two friends were reposing on their blankets near the spring, and when Arthur rode up, they greeted him with a broad grin.

"Well, Colonel," said Frank, "you come near going back to India by a short route, didn't you?"

"Did you ever travel on horseback in such frightful places as this, during your wanderings in Europe?" asked Johnny.

Arthur had, by this time, somewhat recovered from his fright, though his face was still very pale, and he drew a long breath every now and then, when he thought of the dangers he had passed through.

"No," he replied, to Johnny's question. "I never traveled much among the mountains. It always makes my head dizzy, to look down from a height."

"How, then, did you stand it," said Archie, with a sly wink at his companions, "when you were perched upon the 'very top of the middle mast' of your ship, looking out for whales?"

"Eh?" exclaimed Arthur. "Why - I - you know" -

Arthur was cornered. He did not know how to answer this question, so he kneeled down by the spring, and took a drink, in order to gain time to reflect. "I was obliged to stand it," said he, at length, looking up at his companions. "I couldn't help myself. I say, boys," he added, desiring to turn the conversation into another channel, "you've got us into a nice scrape by your cowardice. If you had followed me, those fellows would have been the prisoners now."

At this moment the robber chief approached the group, holding in his hand a sheet of soiled paper and a lead pencil. "Take these," said he, handing the articles to Frank, "and write to your uncle, telling him how matters stand. Say to him that you and your friends are prisoners, that I am going to take you where no one will ever think of looking for you, and that when I am paid eighty thousand dollars in gold, I will set you at liberty, and not before. Tell him, further, that I shall send this note to him by one of my men; and that if he does not return in safety by sunrise to-morrow morning, I will make scarecrows of you."

Frank picked up his saddle-bags, which he used as a desk, and, after borrowing the robber's bowie-knife to sharpen his pencil, he began the letter, and wrote down what Pierre had dictated, using as nearly as possible the chief's own words.

"That's all right," said the latter, when his prisoner had read the letter aloud.

"Now," said Frank, "may I not add a postscript, telling Uncle James that we are well and hearty, and that we have been kindly treated, and so on."

"Certainly; only be careful that you do not advise him to capture my messenger."

Frank again picked up his pencil, and wrote as follows:

"The above was written by Pierre's command, and I have his permission to say a word for ourselves. You need not pay out any money for Archie and me; and I know that if I was allowed an opportunity to talk to Johnny, he would send the same message to his father. We are now in Pass Christian - a difficult place to escape from, but we intend to make the attempt this very night. Detain Pierre's messenger, by all means; then send Dick and Bob with a party of men up here by daylight, and they can capture every one of these villains."

That was what Frank added to the letter, but, when Pierre ordered him to read it, he made up a postscript as he went along; for he knew that if the chief were made acquainted with the real contents of the note, he would not send it. The Ranchero did not know one letter from another, and he was obliged to rely entirely upon Frank, who read:

"We're all hunky-dory thus far. Pierre don't seem to be so bad a fellow, after all; in fact, he's a brick. He treats us like gentlemen; but, of course, we'd rather be at home, so please send on the money for Archie and me, and see that Mr. Harris and Mr. Vane do the same for Johnny and Arthur."

"You're sure, now," said Pierre, as Frank handed him the letter, after addressing it to Mr. Winters, "that you haven't told your uncle where we are, or advised him to try to rescue you?"

"There's the note," replied the prisoner, "and if you think I have been trying to deceive you, read it yourself."

"I guess it's all right," said the chief. "At any rate, I'll run the risk. I have treated you like gentlemen, and if you want me to continue to do so, you must behave yourselves, and not try to play any tricks upon me. Now, mind what I say. If any of you hear the others talking of escape, and don't tell me of it, I'll pitch every one of you into that gully."

Having given utterance to this threat, and emphasized it by scowling savagely at his prisoners, Pierre turned on his heel and walked away.

By this time, dinner was ready, and the boys were invited to sit down and help themselves. The principal dish was dried meat, but there were luxuries in the shape of sandwiches, cakes, crackers, and tea and coffee, which the cook had found in the pack-saddle, and which he did not hesitate to appropriate. The table was the ground under one of the trees, and the grass did duty both as table-cloth and dishes.

"Now, boys," said the chief, "here's a dinner fit for a king. Pitch in, and don't stand upon ceremony."

"I don't think you will find us at all bashful," said Archie, dryly, "seeing that the most of this grub belongs to us."

As the robbers and their prisoners were hungry after their long ride, they fell to work in earnest. Archie sat on his knees in the midst of the group, and, while his teeth were busy upon a sandwich, his eyes wandered from one to another of the Rancheros, and finally rested upon Mr. Mercedes, whose actions instantly riveted his attention. It had evidently been a long time since the robbers had sat down to a respectable dinner, and they all seemed determined to make the most of it - especially Antoine, who devoted his attention entirely to the eatables that had been found in the pack-saddle. He lay stretched out at full length on the ground, one hand being occupied in supporting his head, and the other in transferring the sandwiches from the table to his capacious mouth. Two of the sandwiches would have made a good meal for an ordinary man, unless he was very hungry; but they did not go far toward satisfying the appetite of Mr. Mercedes, for, during the short time that Archie sat looking at him, he put no less than half a dozen out of sight, and seemed to have room for plenty more. Archie began to be alarmed. By the time he could finish one sandwich, Antoine would have swallowed every one on the table, and there would be nothing left but the dried meat.

"Will the small gentleman from Maine be kind enough to pass the plum-pudding - I mean the one that's got the most raisins in it?" said Johnny, who was inclined to be facetious.

"See here, fellows!" exclaimed Archie, and the earnest expression of his countenance arrested the laughing at once. "This is no time for joking. The rule of this boarding-house seems to be, Look out for number one. I intend to do it; and, if you want to get any thing to eat, you had better follow my example."

So saying, he caught up three or four sandwiches, and half a dozen cakes, and started toward the spring, where he sat down to finish his dinner. The other boys comprehended this piece of strategy, and, in less time than it takes to tell it, the table was cleared of every thing except the dried meat. Mr. Mercedes uttered an angry growl, and gazed after Johnny, who had snatched the last sandwich almost out of his hand, and then whipped out his knife, and turned his attention to the meat.

When the robbers had finished their dinner, Pierre held a whispered consultation with one of his men, who, after placing Frank's letter carefully away in the crown of his sombrero, mounted his horse, and rode down the pass. The others, with the exception of a solitary sentinel, sought their blankets, and the boys were left to themselves.

"Now," said Johnny, in a whisper, addressing himself to Frank, "tell us what you wrote in that postscript. You surely did not ask your uncle to send any money for you and Archie?"

"Of course not!" replied Frank. "I, for one, am not worth twenty thousand dollars; and I would rather stay here until I am gray-headed, and live on nothing but dried meat all the while, than ask Uncle James to give twenty cents for me."

"That's the talk," said Johnny, approvingly, while Archie raised himself on his elbow, and patted his cousin on the back. Frank then repeated what he had written in the postscript, as nearly as he could recollect it, and it was heartily indorsed by all the boys, even including Arthur Vane, who said:

"I am glad to see that you are recovering your courage, Frank. If you had all showed a little pluck, when Pierre attacked us this morning, we should not have been in this predicament."

"We'll not argue that point now," said Archie. "Let's talk about our plans for escape. By the way, what sort of fellows do you suppose Pierre takes us for, if he imagines that he can frighten us into carrying tales about one another?"

"I'd like to know, too," said Arthur, sitting up on his blanket, and looking very indignant. "I wonder if he is foolish enough to believe that one of us would tell him, if he heard the others talking of escape! If I thought there was one in this party mean enough to do that, I would never speak to him again."

"Now, don't you be alarmed," said Johnny. "We've been through too much to go back on each other. But how shall we get away? that's the question."

"Let us rush up and knock them down, and pitch them over into the gully," said Arthur. "Follow me; I'll get you out of this scrape."

"We couldn't gain any thing by a fight," said Frank. "Four boys are no match for five grown men."

"I'd give Sleepy Sam if I could only see Dick and Bob poke their noses over some of these rocks around here," said Archie. "They will be after us, as soon as they find out that we are captured; and when they get their eyes on these 'Greasers,' as they call them, there'll be fun."

"But we don't want to wait for them," said Frank. "We must escape to-night, if possible. We can find our way home from here; but, if we stay with these villains two or three days longer, they will have taken us so far into the mountains, that we never can get out. I propose that we wait until dark, and see what arrangements they intend to make for the night, before we determine upon our plans. If they allow us to remain unbound, and leave only one sentinel to guard us, we'll see what can be done. In the meantime, I move that we all take a nap."

The prisoners settled themselves comfortably on their blankets, and, in a few moments, three of them were sleeping soundly, all unconscious of the fact that their wide-awake companion was impatiently awaiting an opportunity to repeat to the robber chief every word of their recent conversation.

"Pierre said, that if any of us heard the others talking of escape, and didn't tell him of it, he would pitch us over that precipice," muttered Arthur. "He looked straight at me when he said it; so I shall take him at his word, and put him on his guard against these fellows. I'll not go back on them - O, no! Johnny Harris didn't call me a coward, did he? And that little spindle-shanked Yankee, and his cousin, didn't insult me, by sending me my hat and gun, and the skin of that wolf, and by telling every body in the settlement that I was frightened out of my senses, without seeing any thing to be frightened at, did they? I'd like to catch that Archie Winters by himself. He's little, and I am sure that I could whip him. I'll pay them all for what they have done to me, and before I get through with them, they will learn, that it is always best to treat a gentleman with respect."

As Arthur said this, he looked contemptuously at his slumbering companions, and then turned his back to them, and went to sleep.

CHAPTER XV

MORE TREACHERY

When Frank awoke, it was nearly dark. The glade was lighted up by a fire, that one of the Rancheros had kindled, and beside which he stood, superintending the cooking of the supper. Archie and Johnny were still sleeping soundly, but Arthur Vane's blanket was empty, and that young gentleman was nowhere to be seen.

Frank raised himself to a sitting posture, rubbed his eyes, and yawned; and then, seeing that the cook was rummaging in the pack-saddle after more luxuries, and judging by that that supper was nearly ready, he shook his companions, and arose to his feet. He went to the spring, and was preparing to wash his hands and face in the little brook that ran across the glade, when his attention was attracted by the sound of voices close by. He found that they came from behind the bowlder; and, after listening a moment, he recognized the voices as those of Pierre Costello, and Arthur Vane. At first, Frank thought nothing of this circumstance. He bent over the brook, and plunged his hands into the water, when the thought occurred to him that this was a strange proceeding on the part of Arthur Vane. If the latter had any thing to say to the chief, why did he not talk to him in the camp? Frank's suspicions were aroused. He stood, for a moment, undecided how to act, and then, dropping on his hands and knees, he crept cautiously around the end of the bowlder, and presently came in sight of Pierre and his companion. They were sitting on the ground, facing each other - the chief calmly smoking a cigarette, while Arthur was amusing himself by cutting the grass around him with the Ranchero's bowie-knife.

"This is very odd," thought Frank. "Arthur acts more like a confidential friend than a prisoner."

Our hero drew back, and listened to the conversation that followed, during which he gained some insight into the character of his new acquaintance.

"I do not admire your way of doing business," he heard Arthur say, at length. "You treat me no better than you treat them. You told me that you knew by my looks that I was a gentleman, and you promised to respect me as such. You assured me that I should be allowed to show fight whenever I pleased, and that you would not hurt me for it. How have you kept those promises? What did you do to me this morning? You jerked my gun out of my hands, and raised it over my head, as if you were going to knock me down. One of your men threw his lasso around my neck, and choked me until I could scarcely breathe, and another aimed a pistol at me. Is that treating me like a gentleman or a visitor?"

"What else could we do?" demanded Pierre. "Didn't you tell me that you wanted us to act natural, so that your three ene-mies would not suspect that you had a previous understanding with me in regard to their capture?"

"Certainly; but I didn't tell you to abuse me, did I? See how I was treated when we were coming through this pass! My keeper struck my horse with his lasso, and came near sending me over the precipice; and you laughed at it. When I look toward you, why don't you give me a wink, or a nod, to show that you have not forgotten your promises, and that you will protect me?"

"Because I never have had a chance to do it without being seen by the others. If you know when you are well off, you will take every precaution to keep those boys from finding out how treacherous you have been. You must not expect any signs of friendship from me. I shall stick to my promise, and see that no serious injury is done you; but, if you will insist in showing your courage by fighting us, you must make up your mind to be roughly handled. You say that Frank didn't read to me what he wrote in that letter?"

"No, he did not. He never said a word to his uncle about sending the money. He told him not to do it. He advised him to capture your messenger, by all means, and to send those trappers up here, with a party of men, by daylight to-morrow morning."

"Well, they'll not find us," said the chief, who seemed to take the matter very coolly. "By daylight we shall be miles from here. We'll start as soon as the moon rises, so that we can see to travel through the pass. After supper, I shall have those fellows bound hand and foot - that will prevent their escape, I think - and, of course, I must tie you, also."

"I don't like the idea of lying all night with my hands fastened behind my back," objected Arthur.

"I can't help that. Those boys must be confined; for I am not going to lose sixty thousand dollars, if I can help it; and, if you wish to avoid suspicion, you must be tied with the rest."

"I shall resist. I want to make those fellows believe that they are a pack of cowards. Don't let your men handle me too roughly."

"I'll look out for that," said Pierre. "Now, let us go back to the camp. You have been away too long already."

"O, you outrageous villain!" thought Frank, who was so astonished and bewildered by what he had heard, that he scarcely knew what he was about. "Won't you suffer for this day's work if we ever get back to the settlement?"

The movements of the traitor, who just then arose to his feet, brought Frank to himself again. He retreated precipitately, and, when Arthur came out from behind the bowlder, he was sitting on his blanket, talking to Archie and Johnny.

"Fellows," said he, in an excited voice, "we're ruined! That rascal has blabbed the whole thing!"

"Who? What rascal? what thing?" asked both the prisoners in a breath. "What's the matter with you?" added Archie, in some alarm, seeing that his cousin wore an exceedingly long face.

"Arthur Vane has just told Pierre that we had made up our minds to escape to-night," replied Frank.

"No!" exclaimed the boys, almost paralyzed by the information.

"It's a fact. After supper, we are to be bound hand and foot; and Arthur, to show how brave he is, and how cowardly we are, is going to resist, and Pierre has promised that his men shall not handle him roughly. O, you'll find out!" he continued, seeing that his friends looked incredulous. "I crept up behind that bowlder, and heard all about it. I did not understand all the conversation; but I know that Arthur is a traitor, and that we are indebted to him for our capture."

Archie and Johnny were utterly confounded. They could not find words strong enough to express their feelings. They sat on their blankets, and looked at each other in blank amazement. Presently, Arthur came in sight, and his appearance served to restore their power of action; and then, for the first time, they seemed to realize the full enormity of the offense of which he had been guilty. Archie jumped to his feet, and commenced pulling off his jacket.

"Fellows," said he, throwing down his sombrero, and rolling up his shirt-sleeves, "I'm going to pound some of the meanness out of him."

"And I'll help you!" exclaimed Johnny, excitedly. "Who ever heard of such a thing?" And Johnny brought his fist down into the palm of his hand, with a noise like the report of a pistol.

"Don't do it, boys!" interposed Frank. "Come here, Archie! Sit down, Johnny. He will be punished enough, when he gets back to the settlement. Let's cut him at once, and have nothing more to do with him. Johnny, put on your jacket! Behave yourself, Archie!"

Frank found it hard work to turn the two boys from their purpose. Their indignation had been thoroughly aroused, and, if Arthur had only known it, he was in a dangerous neighborhood. Although Frank was quite as angry as his friends, he had more prudence. He did not believe that they were the proper ones to execute vengeance upon their enemy. His punishment would come soon enough, and it would be quite as terrible as Arthur was able to bear. By dint of a good deal of coaxing, and pushing, and scolding, he finally got Archie and Johnny on their blankets again, and just then the traitor came up. His face wore a triumphant smile, that was exceedingly irritating to the three boys just then, and he approached them with as much assurance as though he had never in his life been guilty of a mean action.

"I have been out enjoying the cool breeze," said he, not noticing the angry glances that were directed toward him.

"Put it all in, while you are about it," exclaimed Johnny. "Say that you have been holding a consultation with Pierre, in regard to our escape to-night."

Arthur turned very red in the face, and took a step or two backward, as if Johnny had aimed a blow at him; and then, somewhat recovering himself, he opened his eyes, puckered up his lips, and looked from one to the other of his companions, with an expression of intense astonishment.

"How, now, Innocence!" exclaimed Archie. "You're a nice

looking fellow. Go away from here."

"Why, boys," stammered Arthur, "I do not understand you. I have not seen Pierre" -

"Go away!" said Johnny, again rising to his feet - a movement that was instantly imitated by the pugnacious Archie.

"Can't you tell me what's the matter?" demanded Arthur, making a desperate effort to look unconcerned, and to call up some of that courage of which he had so often boasted.

"Have you got the impudence - the brass, to come to us, and ask what's the matter, after what you have done?" asked Archie, angrily. "We'll soon let you know what's" -

"Hold on, boys!" interrupted Frank, who saw that Archie's rage was in a fair way to get the better of him. "Johnny, stand back! Keep still, Archie! Go about your business, Arthur Vane! We know just what passed between you and Pierre, not five minutes ago, and we don't want to listen to any excuses or explanations."

"Explanations!" shouted Archie. "Excuses! for being a traitor!"

"Go over there among those yellow gentlemen," continued Frank. "You are their friend, and there's where you belong. Don't dare come near any of us again. Start!"

"Yes, start - mizzle - clear out!" roared Archie, getting angrier every moment. "Begone! Make yourself scarce about here!"

"Well, I think this is a nice way to treat a gentleman," growled Arthur, as he turned on his heel, and walked slowly away.

"Pick up that blanket and saddle," said Johnny. "Take all your plunder away from here, and remember that this side of the glade belongs to us."

"Yes, remember it - bear it in mind!" exclaimed Archie, who seemed to think it his duty to give emphasis to what the others said. "Think of it continually."

Arthur glared savagely upon Archie; but, fearing to irritate him and his friends further, by refusing to obey their commands, he shouldered his baggage, and walked sullenly toward the fire, around which the Rancheros were congregated, awaiting the summons to supper.

"Benedict Arnold!" said Johnny, as soon as the traitor was out of hearing.

Frank and Archie thought the name appropriate. It clung to Arthur as long as he remained in that part of California.

CHAPTER XVI

THE ESCAPE

Had the huge bowlder in the middle of the glade suddenly burst into a thousand fragments, it could scarcely have created greater consternation than that which filled our three heroes, when they stretched themselves on their blankets, to discuss the treachery of their companion. Of course, the first question that arose was, What object could he have in view? A dozen different opinions were advanced, but none of them were correct. The boys were all satisfied now, that no ransom was to be demanded for Arthur, and they were quite willing to believe that he expected to share in the sixty thousand dollars which Pierre hoped to receive for them. They never imagined that the traitor had been instigated by a desire to be revenged upon them, and that all that had happened to them during the day was the result of the incidents that had transpired during their ride to the old fur-trader's ranch.

"I really believe that Benedict Arnold belongs to this band of outlaws," said Frank. "If he does, that's all the good it will do him, as far as handling any of my uncle's money is concerned. It's lucky that we have found him out."

"It's unfortunate that we didn't find him out long ago," said Archie, who had by this time recovered his usual good nature.

"Our plans for escape are all knocked in the head for this night," continued Frank; "but we will hold ourselves in readiness to seize the first opportunity that is offered. Dick and Bob will be on our trail in a few hours."

At this moment, Pierre entered the glade from the side opposite the spring, and stopped to say a few words to the sentinel, who immediately approached the prisoners, and took his stand within a few paces of them.

"These villains must be afraid of us," said Frank, with a laugh.

"They'd better be," returned Johnny. "I wouldn't like to have sixty thousand dollars wrapped up in such slippery customers as we are."

"I wonder if Pierre thinks we can fly?" said Archie. "That's the only way I can see for getting out of here, while these robbers are all around us. I say, old fellow," he added, turning to the sentinel, "are you a good shot on the wing?"

The Ranchero shrugged his shoulders, and tapped his revolvers significantly.

"I judge from that you are a good shot on the wing," continued Archie. "Let me advise you to keep both eyes open; for the first thing you know, you'll see us disappearing over the tops of these mountains. Each of us has a patent, duplex, double-back-action flying-machine in his pocket."

Archie was going on to explain to the Ranchero the principles on which his imaginary flying-machine operated, when the call to supper interrupted him.

During the meal, the robbers were quite as polite as they had been at dinner. They gobbled up every thing within their reach, devouring it greedily, as though they feared that some-body might get more than his share, and the boys, having learned by experience, that, when one sojourns among Romans, it is a good plan to do as Romans do, snatched what they liked best, and ran back to their blankets.

"Look at Benedict," said Johnny, speaking as plainly as a mouthful of cracker would permit. "He's hot about something."

Arthur was sitting on the ground beside the robber chief, to whom he was talking earnestly, and even angrily, judging by the frantic manner in which he flourished his arms about his head, and struck with his fists at the empty air. Pierre was listening attentively, and so were all the other members of the band, who appeared to be deeply interested in what he was saying. Arthur had told the chief that his secret was discovered, and Pierre had urged him to use every exertion to allay the suspicions of the boys.

"You don't know them as well as I do," said the Ranchero; "and, if you will take my advice, you will try to make friends with them again."

"That's something I'll never do," said Arthur, decidedly. "Shall a gentleman's son stoop to beg the good-will of a lot of young Arabs? Not if he knows himself; and he thinks he does. They have found me out, somehow, and I don't care if they have. I may as well throw off the mask entirely. I'll let them see that, while they are prisoners, and bound hand and foot, I am at liberty to go and come when I please."

When Arthur said this, he was gazing into the fire, and consequently did not see the significant glances which the robber chief exchanged with his men. It might have astonished him to know that he was not free to go and come when he pleased; and that Pierre, in spite of all his promises to the contrary, intended to demand twenty thousand dollars for him, as well as for the others.

When Frank and his friends had eaten their supper, they began to make preparations for the night, by collecting a pile of dried leaves and grass, over which they spread their blankets, placing the saddles at the head of the bed, to serve as pillows. When the couch was completed, it was very inviting, and, had it not been for the knowledge of the fact that they were to be bound hand and foot, they would have been sure of a good night's rest.

Frank could not go to bed without visiting Roderick. He found the horse standing quietly by the spring, and when he saw his master approaching, he raised his head and welcomed him with a shrill neigh.

"O, if we could only get half a minute's start of these robbers!" said Frank, patting the animal's glossy neck, "wouldn't we show them a clean pair of heels? They'd never have us prisoners again, I *bet*."

Frank emphasized the last word by punching Roderick in the ribs with his thumb - an action which caused the animal to lay back his ears, and kick viciously, with both feet, at some imaginary object behind him.

When our hero returned to the place where he had left Archie and Johnny, he saw them lying on their beds securely bound. Pierre stood close by, with a lasso in his hand, and, when Frank came up, he greeted him with a fierce scowl, and, in a savage tone of voice, commanded him to cross his arms behind his back. Frank obeyed, and the Ranchero, while he was busy confining him, inquired:

"Do you remember what I said to you at noon?"

"About what?" asked Frank.

"About making scare-crows of you and your friends, if my messenger does not return at daylight."

"I believe I do remember something about it."

"Then why did you advise your uncle to detain him? You must be tired of life. You told Mr. Winters to send those rascally trappers up here, with a party of men, to capture us."

"Now, see here, Pierre," exclaimed Frank, angrily, "Dick and Bob are not rascals. They are honest men, and what they own, they have worked hard for. They will be up here - you may depend upon that - and, if Dick once gets his hands on you" -

"O, won't he shake him up, though!" cried Archie, from his blanket. "I wouldn't be in Pierre's shoes then for all the money he will ever get for us."

"You may make up your minds to one thing," said the chief; "and that is, if so much as a hair of that messenger's head is harmed, you will be swinging from some of these trees at sunrise."

"That is a soothing story to tell to a person who is trying to go to sleep," observed Johnny.

"You can't make us believe that you would throw away sixty thousand dollars," said Frank. "Be careful," he added, as Pierre, after confining his arms with one end of the lasso, began to wind the other around his ankles; "make those knots secure, or I may get away from you again."

"I'll risk that. Now, good-night, and pleasant dreams to you."

The robber lifted Frank in his arms, and laid him upon his blanket, as if he had been a sack of flour, and then walked off, leaving his prisoners to their meditations. Scarcely had he disappeared, when Arthur, who had stood at a little distance, watching the operations of the chief, came up, and, after regarding the three boys a moment with a smile of triumph, inquired:

"How do you feel now? I hope you will enjoy a good night's rest. You see I am at liberty." And he stretched out his arms, to show that they were not confined.

"Of course," said Frank. "You ought to be; you are one of Pierre's band. We are under obligations to you for what you have done for us."

"How did you find it out?" asked Arthur.

"Why, one of those Arabs you used to know in Patagonia, came up here, and told us how you acted while you were in that country, and we thought it best to keep an eye on you," answered Archie.

"See here, Benedict," said Johnny. "Have you forgotten that we told you to keep your distance?"

"No; but I generally go where I please," replied Arthur.

"You have done something worth boasting of, haven't you?"

"Well - yes; but I am not done with you yet. If I have any influence with Pierre - and I think I have - you'll not see home for a year - perhaps longer."

"Pierre! Pierre!" shouted Archie, suddenly. "I say, Pierre!"

"Well, what's the row?" asked that worthy, from his bed by the fire.

"I'll make you a present of my horse, if you will give me my liberty for just two minutes. Will you do it?"

"I guess not," replied the robber.

"I promise you that I will not attempt any tricks," pleaded Archie. "I only want to show Benedict something. Come, Pierre, that's a good fellow."

The Ranchero laughed, and turned over on his blanket, without making any answer, and Archie, being satisfied that it was useless to urge the matter, laid his head upon his hard pillow, and looked indignantly at the traitor.

"Never mind," said he. "I'll be unbound to-morrow morning, and I'll know how to get up an appetite for breakfast."

Arthur understood what the prisoner meant by getting up an appetite for breakfast, and it made him angry. He was very brave, now. His three enemies were lying before him unable to defend themselves, and it was a fine opportunity to execute vengeance upon them. He suddenly took it into his head that it would be a nice thing to punish them all, beginning with the one who had first excited his animosity.

"Hold on, you little Yankee," said he. "I'll attend to you in a minute. Johnny Harris, what was that name you applied to me?"

"It was a new one we have given you," answered Johnny. "We have called you after the meanest man that ever lived - Benedict Arnold. Do you know him? Did you ever meet him while you were hunting lions and tigers in Europe?"

Frank and his cousin laughed loudly, which so enraged Arthur that he caught up a stick, that happened to be lying near him, and struck Johnny a severe blow with it.

"O, you coward!" shouted Archie, struggling frantically to free his arms. "What do you mean by hitting a man when he is down, and can't move hand or foot?"

The traitor turned fiercely upon Archie, and was about to use the stick upon him, when the gruff voice of the sentinel arrested his hand. The Ranchero pointed toward the fire, and Arthur, understanding the motion, threw down the stick, and walked away, shaking his head, and muttering to himself.

"He had better keep close to his friends to-morrow," said Johnny, his face all wrinkled up with pain.

The other boys thought so too. Each one of them had rather that Arthur had struck him instead of Johnny; for the latter, although high-spirited, and inclined to be belligerent under provocation, was a good-natured, accommodating fellow, who gained hosts of friends wherever he went, and who never hesitated to make any sacrifice for the benefit of others. Frank had never before witnessed such an exhibition of cowardly vindictiveness, and he was almost sorry that he had protected Arthur.

The traitor, well satisfied with what he had done, and only regretting that he had been interrupted before his revenge was complete, spread his blanket beside the chief; and, after that, nothing happened for a long time to disturb the silence of the camp. The Rancheros were soon in a sound sleep, even including Antoine Mercedes, the sentinel, who sat with his back against a tree, his head hung down upon his breast and his right hand, which rested on the ground beside him, grasping a revolver. He had been placed there by his chief to watch the prisoners; but, believing that there was little danger of their escape, and being unwilling to be deprived of his usual rest, he had gone to sleep as soon as the others. The boys, however, were wide awake. The exciting events of the day, and the pain occasioned by their bonds, effectually banished sleep from their eyes, and they passed the long hours in pondering upon what Arthur had done, and trying in vain to find a comfortable position on their blankets. Johnny, especially, was very restless. He lay for a long time watching the sentinel, and thinking how easily he and his companions could effect their escape, if their hands and feet were free; then he wondered if Pierre was in earnest, when he said that he would make "scare-crows" of them if his messenger did not return by daylight; and, finally, he turned over, and tried, for the hundredth time, to go to sleep.

The fire, which was still burning brightly, lighted up every corner of the glade, and, from the new position in which he lay, Johnny could see how Archie's arms were bound. They were crossed behind his back, and the lasso was wrapped twice around them, and tied in a square knot - a single glance at which drove all thoughts of sleep out of Johnny's mind, and suggested to him the idea of an attempt to liberate his friend. The knot, on account of the stiffness of the lasso, had not been drawn very tight, and Johnny thought he had hit upon a plan to untie it.

"Archie," he whispered, excitedly.

"Hallo!" was the response.

"Are you asleep?"

"No; nor am I likely to be to-night," growled Archie. "This lasso hurts me dreadfully. Pierre drew it as tight as he could."

"Don't talk so loud," whispered Johnny. "Keep your eyes on that sentinel, and, if he moves, shake your arms."

"What for?" demanded Archie. "What are you going to do?"

"I don't know that I can do any thing; but I am going to try."

"All right; go ahead."

Johnny took a long look at the Ranchero, to make sure that he was sound asleep, and then, rolling up close to Archie, he went to work with his teeth to untie the lasso, with which the latter's arms were bound. This was not so easy a task as he had imagined it would be; but the knot yielded a little with every pull he made upon it, and, after ten minutes hard work, Johnny rolled back upon his blanket with an expression of great satisfaction upon his countenance, and watched his friend as he unwound the lariat with which his feet were confined.

"Hurrah for you, Johnny!" whispered Archie, a moment afterward. "We'll out-wit these greasers yet. Hold easy, now, and I'll soon give you the free use of your hands and feet."

Archie's fingers made quick work with Johnny's bonds, and,

when he had untied his arms, he left him to do the rest, and turned to release his cousin. This he soon accomplished, and then the three boys, astonished at their success, crept up closer together, to hold a consultation.

"Lead on Frank, and we'll follow," said Johnny.

"I will do the best I can," replied Frank. "Let's stick together as long as possible; but, if we are discovered, we must separate, and let each man take of himself. Remember, now, the one that reaches home must not sleep soundly until the others are rescued."

As Frank said this, he threw himself flat upon the ground, and crawled slowly and noiselessly through the grass, toward the ledge by which they had entered the glade in the morning. They passed the sentinel without arousing him, and approached the fire around which lay the stalwart forms of the Rancheros, who snored lustily, in blissful ignorance of what was going on close by them.

The boys' hearts beat high with hope as they neared the ledge, and Johnny was in the very act of reaching over to give Frank an approving slap on the back, when the movement was arrested by a loud yawn behind him. This was followed by an ejaculation of astonishment, and, an instant afterward, the report of a pistol rang through the glade. The sentinel had just awakened from his sleep, and discovered that the prisoners' blankets were empty.

"Help! help!" he shouted, in stentorian tones, discharging another barrel of his revolver, to arouse his companions. "Pierre, your birds have flown!"

"Run now, fellows!" whispered Frank, and, suiting the action to the word, he jumped up, and took to his heels.

CHAPTER XVII

THE STRUGGLE ON THE CLIFF

As we have before remarked, the place in which the Rancheros had made their camp was a natural recess in the mountains. It was surrounded on three sides by rocky cliffs, the tops of which seemed to pierce the clouds, and whose sides were so steep that a goat could scarcely have found footing thereon. In front of the glade was the gorge, the sight of which had so terrified Arthur Vane, and which was so deep that the roar of the mountain torrent, that ran through it, could be but faintly heard by one standing on the cliffs above.

There were three ways to get out of the glade: one was by the narrow ledge of rocks by which the Rancheros and their captives had entered it in the morning; another was by a path on the opposite side of the glade, which also ran along the very brink of the precipice; the third was by climbing up the cliffs to the dizzy heights above. These avenues of escape were all more or less dangerous, and one unaccustomed to traveling in the mountains would have been at a loss to decide which to take. Indeed, a very timid boy would have preferred to remain a prisoner among the Rancheros, as long as he was sure of kind treatment and plenty to eat, rather than risk any of them. If he took either of the paths that ran along the chasm, he would require the skill of a rope-dancer to cross it in safety; for they were both narrow and slippery, and a single misstep in the darkness would launch him into eternity. If he tried to scale the mountains, which, in some places, overhung the glade, he would be in equal danger; for he might, at any moment, lose his balance, and come tumbling back again.

Frank and his two friends had thought of all these things during the day, and they knew just what perils they were likely to encounter; but they were not formidable enough to turn them from their purpose. While they were crawling cautiously through the grass, they had been allowed ample time to make up their minds what they would do, if their flight should be discovered before they got out of the glade; and, consequently, when the yells of the sentinel, and the reports of his pistol, told them that the pursuit was about to begin, they did not hesitate, but proceeded at once to carry out the plans they had formed. Archie, the moment he jumped to his feet, darted toward the cliffs, while Frank and Johnny ran for the ledge by which they had entered the pass in the morning; and, by the time the Rancheros were fairly awake, their prisoners had disappeared as completely as though they had never been in the glade at all.

Archie had chosen the most difficult way of escape, and he had done so with an object. He believed that, as soon as Pierre and his band became aroused, they would rush in a body for the path that led toward the settlement; and Archie did not like the idea of running a race through the darkness along the brink of that precipice. He might make a misstep, and fall into the gorge, and that would be infinitely worse than remaining a prisoner. His enemies, he thought, would not be likely to follow him up the cliffs; but if they did, and he found that he could not distance them, there were plenty of excellent hiding-places among the bushes and rocks, where he could remain in perfect security, with an army searching for him. Johnny and Frank did not look at the matter in that way. They thought not of concealment; they took the nearest and easiest way home, and trusted entirely to their heels.

"Help! help!" shouted the sentinel, discharging the barrels of his revolver in quick succession. "The boys have gone!"

For a moment, great confusion reigned in the camp. The Rancheros sprang to their feet, and hurried hither and thither, each one asking questions, and giving orders, to which nobody paid the least attention, and the babel of English and Spanish that arose awoke the echoes far and near. The chief was the only one who seemed to know what ought to be done. He examined the beds to satisfy himself that the prisoners had really gone, and then his voice was heard above the tumult, commanding silence.

The first thing he did, when quiet had been restored, was to swear lustily at the sentinel, for allowing the prisoners to escape, and then he set about making preparations for pursuit. He sent two of the band on foot down the path that led toward the settlement, another he ordered to saddle the horses, and the rest he commanded to search every nook and corner of the glade.

As long as the noise continued, Archie worked industriously; and, being a very active fellow, he got up the mountain at an astonishing rate. But as soon as the chief had succeeded in restoring order, he sat down to recover his breath, and to wait until the Rancheros left the glade: for he was fearful that the noise he necessarily made, in working his way through the thick bushes, might direct his enemies in their search.

Although it was pitch dark on the mountainside, Archie could tell exactly what was going on below him. He knew when the two men left the glade, chuckled to himself when he heard the Ranchero, who had been ordered to saddle the horses, growl at the restive animals, and noted the movements of the party who were searching the bushes. He distinctly heard their voices, and he knew that Arthur Vane was with them.

"Do you think they will get away, Joaquin?" he heard the traitor ask.

"That's hard to tell," was the reply. "It depends a good deal upon how long they have been gone. If they get back to the settlement, you had better keep away from there."

"That's so," said Archie, to himself.

"They'll never reach the settlement if I can help it," declared Arthur. "If I get my eyes on one of them, I bet he don't escape. I'll take him prisoner."

Perhaps we shall find that Arthur did "get his eyes on one of them," and we shall see how he kept his promise.

The party went entirely around the glade, passing directly beneath Archie, who held himself in readiness to continue his flight, should they begin to ascend the cliff, and finally one of them called out:

"They're not here, Pierre."

"Mount, then, every one of you," exclaimed the chief. "When you reach the end of the pass, scatter out and search the mountains, thoroughly. Antoine, we have to thank you for the loss of a fortune, you idiot."

Archie heard the Ranchero mutter an angry reply, and then came the tramping of horses as the band rode from the glade. In a few seconds the sound died away in the pass, and the fugitive was left alone. His first impulse was to descend into the glade, mount Sleepy Sam, and follow the robbers. Archie could ride the animal without saddle or bridle as well as he could with them; and he was sure that if he could get but a few feet the start of the Rancheros, his favorite could easily distance them. But he remembered the chief's order for the band to "scatter out," and knowing that every path that led toward the settlement would be closely guarded, and fearing that he might run against some of his enemies in the dark, he decided that the safest plan was to remain upon the cliffs, where he could not be followed by mounted men. It cost him a struggle to abandon his horse, which was galloping about the glade, and neighing disconsolately, but he wisely concluded that twenty thousand dollars were worth more to his uncle than Sleepy Sam was to him; and drawing in a long breath, he tightened his sash about his waist, and again began the ascent.

His progress was necessarily slow and laborious, for, in some places, the cliff was quite perpendicular, and the only way he could advance at all, was by drawing himself up by the grass and bushes that grew out of the crevices of the rocks. Sometimes these gave way beneath his weight, and then Archie would descend the mountain for a short distance much more rapidly than he had gone up. He was often badly bruised by these falls. The bushes and the sharp points of the rocks tore his clothing, and it was not long before he was as ragged as any beggar he had ever seen in the streets of his native city.

"By gracious!" exclaimed Archie, stopping for the hundredth time to rest, and feeling of a severe bruise on his cheek which he had received in his last fall, "I am completely tired out. And this is all the work of that Benedict Arnold! Didn't I say that we should see trouble with that fellow? If I were out on clear ground, and had my horse and gun, I'd be willing to forgive him for what he has done to me, but I'll always remember that he struck Johnny over the head, when he was tied, and could not defend himself."

Wiping the big drops of perspiration from his forehead, and panting loudly after his violent exertions, Archie again toiled up the mountain, so weary that he could scarcely drag one foot after the other. He stumbled over logs, fell upon the rocks, and dragged himself through bushes that cut into his tattered garments like a knife. Hour after hour passed in this way, and, finally, just as the sun was rising, Archie, faint with thirst, aching in every joint, and bleeding from numerous wounds, stepped upon a broad, flat bowlder, which formed the summit of the cliff.

On his right, between him and a huge rock that rose for fifty feet without a single break or crevice, was a narrow but deep chasm which ran down the cliff he had just ascended, and into which he had more than once been in imminent danger of falling as he stumbled about in the darkness. Far below him was the glade, a thin wreath of smoke rising from the smouldering camp-fire, and on his left was the gorge, a hundred times more frightful in his eyes now than it had ever seemed before. In front of him the mountain sloped gently down to the valley below, its base clothed with a thick wood, which at that height looked like an unbroken mass of green sward, and beyond that, so far away that it could be but dimly seen, was a broad expanse of prairie, from which arose the whitewashed walls of his uncle's rancho. It was a view that would have put an artist into ecstasies, but the fugitive was in no mood to appreciate it. He had no eye for the beauties of nature then - he had other things to think of; and he regarded the picturesque mountains and rocks, and the luxuriant woods, as so many grim monsters that stood between him and his home.

But Archie could not remain long inactive. After all the dangers he had incurred, and the bruises and scratches he had received, he had accomplished but little. He was still thirty miles from home, hungry and thirsty, and pursued by crafty enemies, who might even then be watching him from some secret covert.

"Oh, if I were only there!" said he, casting a longing glance toward the rancho, whose inmates, just then sitting down to a dainty breakfast, little dreamed how much good a small portion of their bounty would have done the fugitive on the mountain-top. "But, as the rancho can't come to me, I must go to it."

Archie found the descent of the mountain comparatively easy. There were not so many bushes and logs to impede his progress, the slope was more gradual, and he had not gone more than half a mile when he found a cool spring bubbling out from under the rocks. He bathed his hands and face, drank a little of the water, and when he set out again he felt much refreshed. He followed the course of the stream, which ran from the spring down the mountain, keeping a bright lookout for enemies all the while, and stopping now and then to listen for sounds of pursuit, when suddenly, as he came around the base of a rock, he found himself on the brink of the gorge, and confronted by a figure in buckskin, who stood leaning on a long, double-barrel shot-gun. Archie started back in dismay, and so did the boy in buckskin, who turned pale, and gazed at the fugitive as if he were hardly prepared to believe that he was a human being. He speedily recovered himself, however, and after he had let down the hammer of his gun, which he had cocked when the ragged apparition first came in sight, he dropped the butt of the weapon to the ground, exclaiming:

"Archie Winters!"

"Benedict Arnold!"

For a moment the two boys stood looking at each other without moving or speaking. Archie was wondering if it were possible for him to effect the capture of the traitor, and Arthur, while he gazed in astonishment at the fugitive's tattered garments and bloody face, was chuckling to himself, and enjoying beforehand the punishment he had resolved to inflict upon Archie. The opportunity he had wished for so long had arrived at last.

"I have found you, have I?" said Arthur, resting his elbows on the muzzle of his gun, and looking at Archie with a triumphant smile.

"Well, suppose you have; what do you propose to do about it?"

"It is my intention to teach you to respect a gentleman the next time you meet one."

"How are you going to do it?"

"In the first place, by giving you a good beating."

"Humph!" said Archie, contemptuously, looking at Arthur from head to foot, as if he were taking his exact measure. "It requires a boy with considerable 'get up' about him to do that."

"None of your impudence, you little Yankee," exclaimed Arthur, angrily. "I'm going to take some of it out of you before you are two minutes older."

When the traitor selected Archie as the one upon whom he could wreak his vengeance without danger to himself, he had made a great mistake. Archie was smaller than most boys of his age, but, after all, he was an antagonist not to be despised. He was courageous, active, and as wiry as an eel; and his body, hardened by all sorts of violent exercise, was as tough as hickory. He trembled a little when he looked over into the gorge, and thought of the possible consequences of an encounter on that cliff, but he was not the one to save himself by taking to his heels, nor did it come natural to him to stand still and take a whipping as long as he possessed the strength to defend himself. A single glance was enough to convince him that the traitor was in earnest, and Archie watched the opportunity to begin the struggle himself.

"Yes, sir," continued Arthur, "I've got you now just where I want you. I am going to settle this little difference between us, and then I shall take you back to Pierre. If you have any apologies to make, I am willing to listen to them."

The effect of these words not a little astonished the traitor. He had been sure that Archie would be terribly frightened, and that he would either seek safety in flight, or beg hard for mercy; consequently, he was not prepared for what really happened. Scarcely had Arthur ceased speaking, when the place where Archie was standing became suddenly vacant, and, before the traitor could move a finger, his gun was torn from his grasp and pitched over the cliff into the gorge. As the weapon fell whirling through the air, both barrels were discharged, and the reports awoke a thousand echoes, which reverberated among the mountains like peals of thunder.

"Now we are on equal terms," exclaimed Archie, as he clasped the traitor around the body and attempted to throw him to the ground. "You remember that you struck Johnny last night, when he was bound, hand and foot, and couldn't defend himself, don't you?"

"Yes; and now I am going to serve you worse than that," replied Arthur, who, although surprised and taken at great disadvantage by the suddenness of the attack, struggled furiously, and to such good purpose that he very soon broke Archie's hold; "I am going to fling you over the cliff after that gun."

The contest that followed was carried on on the very edge of the precipice, and was long and desperate. Archie, bruised and battered in a hundred places, and weary with a night's travel, was scarcely a match for the fresh and vigorous Arthur, who, in his blind rage, seemed determined to fulfill his threat of throwing him over the cliff after the gun. Fortune favored first one and then the other; but Archie's indomitable courage and long wind carried the day, and he finally succeeded in bearing his antagonist to the ground and holding him there.

"You are not going to throw me over, are you?" gasped Arthur, who was humble enough, now that he had been worsted.

"Do you take me for a savage?" panted Archie, in reply. "I simply wanted to save myself from a whipping that I did not deserve, and I've done it. Now you must go to the settlement with me, to" -

"Here you are!" exclaimed a familiar voice. "Let us see if you will escape me again."

Archie looked up, and saw Antoine Mercedes advancing upon him.

CHAPTER XVIII

CONCLUSION

Archie had been so fully occupied with the traitor that he had not thought of his other enemies, and for a moment he lay upon the ground beside his antagonist, gazing at Antoine in speechless amazement. Resistance, of course, was not to be thought of, and it also seemed useless to make any attempts at escape; for he had been so nearly exhausted by his struggle with Arthur, that he scarcely possessed the power to rise from the ground. "I am caught easy enough," thought he, "and I might as well give up first as last."

"I see before me twenty thousand dollars," said Antoine, hastily coiling up his lasso as he approached.

These words acted like a spur upon Archie's flagging spirits. He no longer thought of surrender: on the contrary, almost before he knew it, he found himself on his feet and going down the mountain like the wind.

"*Carrajo!*" yelled the Ranchero, swinging his lasso around his head.

Archie was afraid of that lasso, for he knew that he was in danger as long as he was within reach of it; but fortunately he had been too quick for Antoine. He heard the lariat whistle through the air behind him, and snap like a whip close to his ear, and then he knew that his enemy had missed his mark.

"Santa Maria!" shouted the robber. "Stop, you young vagabond, or I'll shoot you."

The fugitive was not frightened by this threat. He was not afraid of being shot, nor did he believe that he could be overtaken in a fair race; for, now that he got started, he found that he had wind enough left for a long run. He had lived among the Rancheros long enough to know that they were very poor marksmen, and that they could not boast of their swiftness of foot; and, having escaped the lasso, his spirits rose again, and hope lent him wings. He heard Antoine crushing through the bushes in pursuit, but the sound grew fainter and fainter as he sped on his way. He jumped over rocks and logs, and cleared ravines that at almost any other time would have effectually checked his progress, and when he reached the thick woods at the base of the mountains, the Ranchero was out of sight and hearing.

Archie was well aware of the fact that he had now reached the most dangerous part of his route homeward. The chief had ordered the band to "scatter out" when they reached the end of the pass, and he knew that every road that led toward the settlement was closely watched. He knew, also, that his only chance for escape was to avoid these roads and keep in the thickest part of the woods. He sat down behind some bushes to rest for a few moments, and then started on again, sometimes creeping on his hands and knees, making use of every log and rock to cover his retreat, and stopping frequently to examine the woods in front of him, and to listen for sounds of pursuit. He had accomplished about a mile in this way, when he found himself in one of the numerous bridle-paths that ran through the mountains in every direction, and, what was worse, he saw the scowling visage of Pierre Costello arise from behind a log not ten paces from him. With the same glance he saw something else; and that was a crouching figure in buckskin, which was creeping stealthily toward the robber.

"Here's one caught," said Pierre, stepping into the path and walking toward Archie. "None of your tricks, now; you can't escape."

"I don't intend to try," replied Archie, with a boldness that astonished the robber. "Your game is up, Mr. Pierre, and I advice you to surrender quietly, if you don't want to get hurt!"

"What!" exclaimed the Ranchero. "Surrender! If you know what you are about, you will not offer any resistance. I am a desperate man."

The robber spoke these words boldly enough, but he evidently did not like the looks of things. He gazed earnestly at Archie, as if trying to determine what it was that had encouraged him to show so bold a front, and seeing that he held one hand behind him, Pierre came to the conclusion that he must, by some means, have secured possession of a revolver.

"Drop that weapon, and hold your arms above your head," said the robber.

Archie did not move. While he appeared to be looking steadily at the chief, he was really watching the movements of the figure in buckskin, which had all this while been working its way quickly, but noiselessly, through the bushes, and had now approached within a few feet of the Ranchero.

"Did you hear what I said?" demanded the latter, placing his hand on one of his revolvers. "You are my prisoner."

"Well, then, why don't you come and take me?" asked Archie.

At this moment a slight rustling in the leaves caught the quick ear of the robber, who turned suddenly, uttered a cry of alarm, and fled down the path, closely followed by something that to Archie looked like a gray streak, so swiftly did it move. But it was not a gray streak - it was Dick Lewis, who, after a few of his long strides, collared the Ranchero with one hand and threw him to the ground, and with the other seized the revolver he was trying to draw, and wrested it from his grasp.

Pierre struggled desperately, but to no purpose, for the trapper handled him as easily as though he had been a child.

"Now, then, you tarnal Greaser," exclaimed Dick, "your jig's danced, an' you must settle with the fiddler. If I only had you out on the prairie, I'd larn you a few things I reckon you never heern tell on. Come here, you keerless feller, an' tell me if you 'member what I said to you yesterday! Whar's Frank?"

Before Archie had time to reply, an incident happened, which, had the trapper been a less experienced man than he was, would have turned his triumph into defeat very suddenly. He had more than one enemy to contend with, and the first intimation he had of the fact, was a sound that Archie had heard so often since his residence in California that it had become familiar to him - the whistling noise made by a lariat in its passage through the air. Before Archie could look around to discover whence this new danger came, he saw the trapper stretched at full length on the ground. For an instant his heart stood still; but it was only for an instant, for Dick was on his feet again immediately, and Archie drew a long breath of relief when he saw the lasso, which he feared had settled around his friend's neck, glide harmlessly over his shoulder. The trapper, from force of long habit, was always on the watch for danger, and when he heard that whistling sound in the air, he did not stop to look for his enemy, but dropped like a flash to avoid the lasso; and when he arose to his feet his long rifle was leveled at a thicket of bushes in front of him.

"Show yourself, Greaser!" cried Dick.

The concealed enemy obeyed without an instant's hesitation, and when he stepped into the path, Archie saw that it was Antoine Mercedes.

"Thar's nothin' like knowin' the tricks of the varmints," said Dick, coolly, as he handed his rifle to Archie, and proceeded to disarm Antoine. "If I had been a greenhorn, I should have been well-nigh choked to death by this time; but a man who has seed prairy life, soon larns that his ears was made for use as well as his eyes. Now, little un, whar's the rest of them fellers?"

While the trapper was engaged in confining his prisoners' arms with their own lassos, Archie gave him a rapid account of all that had happened during his captivity, dwelling with a good deal of emphasis on the treachery of Arthur Vane. Dick opened his eyes in astonishment, and, when Archie had finished his story, declared that they would be serving Arthur right if they were to leave him among the robbers.

"Why, he doesn't want to get away from them," said Archie. "He is with them now, hunting for us. He and I had a fight not half an hour ago, and, if Antoine had only stayed away a few minutes longer, Arthur would have been a prisoner too."

At this moment, a party of Rancheros galloped up, led by Uncle James and Mr. Harris, and accompanied by the dogs, which the boys - who had intended to devote the most of their time to stalking the elks, which were abundant in the mountains - had left at home. Marmion and Carlo made every demonstration of joy at seeing Archie once more, and Mr. Winters greeted him as though he had not met him for years.

Without any unnecessary delay, a trusty herdsman was dismounted, and sent back to the ranch with the prisoners, and Archie mounted his horse.

"You had better go home," said Mr. Winters, looking at his nephew's rags and bruises.

"Oh no, uncle," said Archie, quickly. "I promised Frank and Johnny that, if I succeeded in getting away, I wouldn't sleep until they were safe among friends. I want to go with you."

Uncle James did not urge the matter, and Dick, although he shook his head at Archie, and called him a "keerless feller," was proud of his pluck.

The trapper, who was the acknowledged leader of the party, set out at a rapid trot toward the pass, but had not gone far, when he stopped, and turned his head on one side to listen. "Spread out, fellers," said he, waving his hand toward the bushes on each side of him. "Thar's something comin'."

The horsemen separated, and took up their positions on each side of the path. They could hear nothing but the chirping of the birds, and the sighing of the wind through the branches above their heads; but they had not been long in their concealments before they found that Dick had not been deceived. The clatter of a horse's hoofs on the hard path, faint and far off at first, but growing louder as the animal approached, came to their ears, and presently Roderick appeared in sight. The first thing Archie noticed was, that he wore neither saddle nor bridle; the second, that he carried Frank and Johnny on his back. One of Frank's hands was twisted in the horse's mane, and his body was tightly clasped in the arms of Johnny, who sat behind him. Archie had never seen the mustang run so swiftly before, and he made up his mind that, if any of the Rancheros were pursuing him, they might as well give up the chase. He also thought that Frank and Johnny would enjoy a long ride before they got a chance to put their feet on the ground again; for Roderick was plainly stampeded. It was fortunate that Dick had sent them into the bushes; for, had the party been in the path then, some of them would have been run down, and, perhaps, trampled to death.

"Out of the way there, Greaser!" shouted Frank, when he discovered the trapper standing in the path.

Dick was not a Greaser; but he thought it best to get out of the way; and Frank would have gone by him, had not Carlo and Marmion recognized their masters, and set up a howl of welcome.

"Whoa!" shouted Johnny and Frank, in concert, and Roderick stopped so suddenly that both his riders were thrown forward on his neck.

"Come here, you boy that fit that ar' Greaser, an' tell me all about it, to onct," exclaimed Dick. "Be they follerin' you?"

"Not that we know of. We haven't seen any of them since daylight. Lend me your lasso, Carlos, and we'll go back and hunt up Archie."

But Archie was already found, and when he rode out of the bushes, Frank was relieved of a great deal of anxiety. He had not seen his cousin since he left the glade, and he feared that he had been re-captured; or, what was worse, had slipped off the ledge into the gorge.

A consultation was now held, and, after Uncle James and Mr. Harris had listened to the boys' story, they decided that it would be a waste of time to search for Arthur Vane. The latter's conduct had induced the belief that he was a friend of the robbers, and could go and come when he pleased. No doubt, when he got tired of life in the mountains, he would return home of his own free will. The party would keep on to the glade, however, and recover Sleepy Sam, and the boys' weapons. When this had been decided upon, Dick's horse, which he had hidden in the bushes, was brought out for Johnny, a lasso was twisted around Roderick's lower jaw, to serve as a bridle, and then the trapper shouldered his long rifle, and gave another exhibition of his "travelin' qualities." He kept the horses in a steady gallop, sometimes "letting out" a little on getting far in advance of them, and, when he stopped at the entrance to the pass, he seemed as fresh as ever.

The boys had expressed the hope that they would surprise some of the robbers in the glade, but were disappointed. They found their saddles, bridles, blankets, and weapons, however, and Archie recovered his horse, which was standing contentedly beside the spring, half asleep, as usual. Every thing was gathered up, including a few articles the robbers had left behind, and, as they rode toward the settlement, the boys told each other that the next time they went hunting, after Pierre's band had all been captured, they would camp in the glade.

Archie was confined to the house for a day or two after that; but, if his body was stiff and bruised, his tongue was all right, and it was a long time before he got through relating the incidents of his fight with the traitor.

Frank and Johnny had met with no adventures, not having seen any of the band after they left the glade. They crossed the ledge without accident - although they confessed that they would think twice before trying it again - and, when they reached the end of the pass, they concealed themselves in a hollow log until morning. When they were about to continue their flight, they discovered the mustang, which, unwilling to be left alone in the glade, had crossed the ledge, and was on his way home. Frank easily caught him; but, knowing his favorite's disposition as well as he did, hesitated about requiring him to carry double; however, he finally decided that Roderick was large enough and strong enough to carry them both, and that he must do it, or take the consequences. Frank thereupon mounted the animal, Johnny climbed up behind him, and Roderick, after a few angry kicks, consented to the arrangement. Believing the boldest course to be the safest, they put the horse to the top of his speed, trusting to his momentum to overcome any thing that might endeavor to obstruct the path.

While Archie was confined to the house, Dick and old Bob were busy, and their efforts were rewarded by the capture of three more of the band, who were sent to San Diego with the others. Only one was left now, and that was Joaquin, who had thus far successfully eluded pursuit. The traitor was also missing; and, although Mr. Vane kept his herdsmen in the mountains continually, nothing had been seen of him. Arthur was paying the penalty of his treachery, and was being punished in a way he had not thought of. After his unsuccessful attempt to capture Archie Winters, he went down the mountain to the place where he had left his horse, and there he found Joaquin, who had narrowly escaped a ball from the rifle of old Bob Kelly. He was in ill-humor about something, but his face brightened when he discovered Arthur.

"We must be off at once," said he. "The mountains are full of men."

"I believe I'll go home," replied Arthur. "I am going to ask my father to give me money enough to take me back to Kentucky; for, of course, I can't live here after what I have done. Before I go, however, I want to tell you, that you and your friends are a set of blockheads. If I had known that you would be so stupid as to allow those fellows to escape, I shouldn't have had any thing to do with you. Good-by, Joaquin."

"Not quite so fast, my lad," said the Ranchero, seizing Arthur's horse by the bridle. "You are worth as much to us as the others."

"What do you mean?" exclaimed Arthur.

"I mean that you are a prisoner, and that you must stay here with us. I hope you understand that?"

Arthur was thunderstruck. "Why, Joaquin," said he, "Pierre promised me faithfully that I should be treated as a visitor, and that no ransom should be demanded for me."

"And did you put any faith in that promise? When your father gives us twenty thousand dollars, you can go, and not before."

Arthur cried, begged, and threatened in vain. Joaquin was firm, and the traitor was obliged to accompany him to the mountains. That night he wrote to his father, informing him of his situation, and Joaquin, after tying his prisoner to a tree, and gagging him, to prevent him from shouting for assistance, rode to the settlement, and left the note on Mr. Vane's doorstep.

During the three weeks following, Arthur led a most miserable life. He had nothing to eat but dried meat, and but little of that. His captor treated him very harshly, tying him to a tree every night, to prevent his escape, and moving him about in the day-time, from place to place, to avoid capture. It soon became known in the settlement, that Arthur was held as a prisoner, and the search was conducted with redoubled energy. Joaquin was constantly on the alert, but he was caught at last; for, one day, just as he and Arthur were about to sit down to their dinner of dried meat, Frank, Archie, and Johnny suddenly appeared in sight, accompanied by the two trappers. Archie had repeatedly declared that he owed the traitor a debt, which he intended to settle the very first time he met him; but when he saw what a wretched condition Arthur was in, he relented, and pitied him from the bottom of his heart.

Joaquin was sent to San Diego to be dealt with according to law, and Arthur went home. He did not remain there long; but, as soon as he was able to travel, started for Kentucky, and every one was glad that he had gone.

Frank and Archie could tell stories now that were worth listening to. They had seen exciting times since their arrival in California, had been the heroes of some thrilling adventures, and they never got weary of talking over the incidents that transpired during their captivity AMONG THE RANCHEROS.

Choose from Thousands of 1stWorldLibrary Classics By

A. M. Barnard
Ada Leverson
Adolphus William Ward
Aesop
Agatha Christie
Alexander Aaronsohn
Alexander Kielland
Alexandre Dumas
Alfred Gatty
Alfred Ollivant
Alice Duer Miller
Alice Turner Curtis
Alice Dunbar
Ambrose Bierce
Amelia E. Barr
Amory H. Bradford
Andrew Lang
Andrew McFarland Davis
Andy Adams
Anna Sewell
Annie Besant
Annie Hamilton Donnell
Annie Payson Call
Annonaymous
Anton Chekhov
Arnold Bennett
Arthur Conan Doyle
Arthur M. Winfield
Arthur Ransome
Atticus
B.H. Baden-Powell
B. M. Bower
Baroness Emmuska Orczy
Baroness Orczy
Basil King
Bayard Taylor
Ben Macomber
Bertha Muzzy Bower
Bjornstjerne Bjornson
Booth Tarkington
Boyd Cable
Bram Stoker
C. Collodi
C. E. Orr
C. M. Ingleby
Carolyn Wells
Catherine Parr Traill
Charles A. Eastman
Charles Dickens

Charles Dudley Warner
Charles Farrar Browne
Charles Ives
Charles Kingsley
Charles Klein
Charles Amory Beach
Charles Hanson Towne
Charles Lathrop Pack
Charles Whibley
Charles Willing Beale
Charlotte M. Braeme
Charlotte M. Yonge
Charlotte Perkins Stetson
Clair W. Hayes
Clarence Day Jr.
Clarence E. Mulford
Clemence Housman
Confucius
Cornelis DeWitt Wilcox
Cyril Burleigh
D. H. Lawrence
Daniel Defoe
David Garnett
Dinah Craik
Don Carlos Janes
Donald Keyhoe
Dorothy Kilner
Dougan Clark
Douglas Fairbanks
E. Nesbit
E.P.Roe
E. Phillips Oppenheim
Earl Barnes
Edgar Rice Burroughs
Edith Van Dyne
Edith Wharton
Edward J. O'Biren
Edward S. Ellis
Edwin L. Arnold
Eleanor Atkins
Eliot Gregory
Elizabeth Gaskell
Elizabeth McCracken
Elizabeth Von Arnim
Ellem Key
Emerson Hough
Emilie F. Carlen
Emily Dickinson
Enid Bagnold

Enilor Macartney Lane
Erasmus W. Jones
Ernie Howard Pie
Ethel Turner
Ethel Watts Mumford
Eugenie Foa
Eugene Wood
Eustace Hale Ball
Evelyn Everett-green
Everard Cotes
F. H. Cheley
F. J. Cross
Federick Austin Ogg
Ferdinand Ossendowski
Francis Bacon
Francis Darwin
Frances Hodgson Burnett
Frances Parkinson Keyes
Frank Gee Patchin
Frank Harris
Frank Jewett Mather
Frank L. Packard
Frank V. Webster
Frederic Stewart Isham
Frederick Trevor Hill
Frederick Winslow Taylor
Friedrich Kerst
Friedrich Nietzsche
Fyodor Dostoyevsky
G.A. Henty
G.K. Chesterton
Gabrielle E. Jackson
Garrett P. Serviss
Gaston Leroux
George A. Warren
George Ade
Geroge Bernard Shaw
George Durston
George Ebers
George Eliot
George Gissing
George MacDonald
George Meredith
George Orwell
George Sylvester Viereck
George Tucker
George W. Cable
George Wharton James
Gertrude Atherton

Grace E. King
Grace Gallatin
Grant Allen
Guillermo A. Sherwell
Gulielma Zollinger
Gustav Flaubert
H. A. Cody
H. B. Irving
H.C. Bailey
H. G. Wells
H. H. Munro
H. Irving Hancock
H. Rider Haggard
H. W. C. Davis
Hamilton Wright Mabie
Hans Christian Andersen
Harold Avery
Harold McGrath
Harriet Beecher Stowe
Harry Houidini
Helent Hunt Jackson
Helen Nicolay
Hendrik Conscience
Hendy David Thoreau
Henri Barbusse
Henrik Ibsen
Henry Adams
Henry Ford
Henry Frost
Henry James
Henry Jones Ford
Henry Seton Merriman
Henry W Longfellow
Herbert A. Giles
Herbert N. Casson
Herman Hesse
Homer
Honore De Balzac
Horace Walpole
Horatio Alger Jr.
Howard Pyle
Howard R. Garis
Hugh Lofting
Hugh Walpole
Humphry Ward
Ian Maclaren
Inez Haynes Gillmore
Irving Bacheller
Israel Abrahams
Ivan Turgenev
J.G.Austin

J. Henri Fabre
J. M. Barrie
J. Macdonald Oxley
J. S. Fletcher
J. S. Knowles
J. Storer Clouston
Jack London
Jacob Abbott
James Allen
James Andrews
James Baldwin
James DeMille
James Joyce
James Lane Allen
James Lane Allen
James Oliver Curwood
James Oppenheim
James Otis
James R. Driscoll
Jane Austen
Janet Aldridge
Jens Peter Jacobsen
Jerome K. Jerome
John Burroughs
John Cournos
John F. Kennedy
John Gay
John Glasworthy
John Habberton
John Joy Bell
John Kendrick Bangs
John Milton
John Philip Sousa
Jonas Lauritz Idemil Lie
Jonathan Swift
Joseph A. Altsheler
Joseph Carey
Joseph Conrad
Joseph E. Badger Jr
Joseph Hergesheimer
Joseph Jacobs
Jules Vernes
Julian Hawthrone
Julie A Lippmann
Justin Huntly McCarthy
Kakuzo Okakura
Kenneth Grahame
Kenneth McGaffey
Kate Langley Bosher
Kate Langley Bosher
Katherine Cecil Thurston

Katherine Stokes
L. A. Abbot
L. T. Meade
L. Frank Baum
Latta Griswold
Laura Lee Hope
Laurence Housman
Lawrence Beasley
Leo Tolstoy
Leonid Andreyev
Lewis Carroll
Lewis Sperry Chafer
Lilian Bell
Lloyd Osbourne
Louis Hughes
Louis Tracy
Louisa May Alcott
Lucy Fitch Perkins
Lucy Maud Montgomery
Lydia Miller Middleton
Lyndon Orr
M. Corvus
M. H. Adams
Margaret E. Sangster
Margaret Vandercook
Margret Penrose
Maria Edgeworth
Maria Thompson Daviess
Mariano Azuela
Marion Polk Angellotti
Mark Overton
Mark Twain
Mary Austin
Mary Catherine Crowley
Mary Cole
Mary Hastings Bradley
Mary Roberts Rinehart
Mary Rowlandson
M. Wollstonecraft Shelley
Maud Lindsay
Max Beerbohm
Myra Kelly
Nathaniel Hawthrone
Nicolo Machiavelli
O. F. Walton
Oscar Wilde
Owen Johnson
P.G. Wodehouse
Paul and Mabel Thorne
Paul G. Tomlinson
Paul Severing

Percy Brebner
Peter B. Kyne
Plato
R. Derby Holmes
R. L. Stevenson
R. S. Ball
Rabindranath Tagore
Rahul Alvares
Ralph Bonehill
Ralph Henry Barbour
Ralph Victor
Ralph Waldo Emmerson
Rene Descartes
Rex Beach
Rex E. Beach
Richard Harding Davis
Richard Jefferies
Richard Le Gallienne
Robert Barr
Robert Frost
Robert Gordon Anderson
Robert L. Drake
Robert Lansing
Robert Lynd
Robert Michael Ballantyne
Robert W. Chambers
Rosa Nouchette Carey
Rudyard Kipling
Samuel B. Allison

Samuel Hopkins Adams
Sarah Bernhardt
Sarah C. Hallowell
Selma Lagerlof
Sherwood Anderson
Sigmund Freud
Standish O'Grady
Stanley Weyman
Stella Benson
Stephen Crane
Stewart Edward White
Stijn Streuvels
Swami Abhedananda
Swami Parmananda
T. S. Ackland
T. S. Arthur
The Princess Der Ling
Thomas A. Janvier
Thomas A Kempis
Thomas Anderton
Thomas Bailey Aldrich
Thomas Bulfinch
Thomas De Quincey
Thomas H. Huxley
Thomas Hardy
Thomas More
Thornton W. Burgess
U. S. Grant
Valentine Williams

Various Authors
Vaughan Kester
Victor Appleton
Virginia Woolf
Walter Camp
Walter Scott
Washington Irving
Wilbur Lawton
Wilkie Collins
Willa Cather
Willard F. Baker
William Dean Howells
William le Queux
W. Makepeace Thackeray
William W. Walter
Winston Churchill
Yei Theodora Ozaki
Yogi Ramacharaka
Young E. Allison
Zane Grey